A Treache

MW00414338

A Chocolate Centered Cozy Mystery Series

Cindy Bell

ISBN-13: 978-1530827084

ISBN-10: 1530827086

Table of Contents

Chapter One 1

Chapter Two 20

Chapter Three 40

Chapter Four 65

Chapter Five 82

Chapter Six 92

Chapter Seven 104

Chapter Eight 122

Chapter Nine 144

Chapter Ten.. 152

Chapter Eleven 164

Chapter Twelve... 177

Chapter Thirteen... 187

Chapter Fourteen 196

Chapter Fifteen 204

Chapter Sixteen 233

Chocolate Cookie Recipe 238

More Cozy Mysteries by Cindy Bell 241

Chapter One

The pungent odor that wafted from the nearby farm was a mixture of freshly cut grass, rich wet soil, and of course the cows that populated the dairy farm. To Ally it smelled just like home. She had often gone to the farm on field trips as a child in order to see what farmers did to maintain their crops and products. Although Ally respected the hard work that a farmer put in, she decided the first time she stepped in a cow patty that she was not the farming type.

Every year Tyler Wolson hosted a farmer's market for the community of Mainbry, the small town that neighbored Blue River. Everyone in the county was invited. It was his way of giving back, and also generating some extra sales for the eggs and milk that he sold. Many of the local shops hosted a booth, including 'Charlotte's Chocolate Heaven'.

Ally layered another pile of the chocolate

cookies she and her grandmother had prepared that morning. These exact cookies weren't something they normally sold, but they baked them specifically for the farmer's market as they held up better in the warm air than many of their other products, and the packaging allowed them to advertise the shop. Ally designed a special small menu that she had printed on the back of the bags that they packaged the cookies in, so that anyone who bought the cookies would know what else they sold. In the bustle of the morning preparation Ally's cat, Peaches, and her grandmother's pot-bellied pig, Arnold, were overlooked. As a result they were both rather uncontrollable in the booth. When Ally almost tripped over Arnold for the fourth time she sighed and growled at the same time.

"Mee-Maw, we have to get this pig out of here. He's going to knock me right off my feet."

"Oh now now, be careful how you talk to Arnold. You know how delicate his feelings are."

"I'm aware." Ally frowned and reached down

to pat the top of the pig's head. "No offense, Arnold, but I really don't want to trip and fall on this giant pile of cookies."

"Oh, that would be bad." Charlotte laughed. "Once we get everything settled I'll take him for a walk, don't worry."

"Thanks." Ally went behind the booth and took a moment to scratch the back of Peaches' ears. The cat was content to be in her carrier in a corner of the booth. She had a reputation for escaping and exploring and Ally was concerned she might get stepped on by a cow if she wandered too far. As she placed the last package of cookies on the pile she took a deep breath and started to relax. It was hard for her not to get anxious over everything being in just the right place. Since she had taken over as manager of her grandmother's chocolate shop, she pressured herself to do a great job. Her grandmother, as always, was there trying to keep her calm.

"Ally, you've done a beautiful job. I'm really impressed with the packaging."

"Thanks Mee-Maw." Ally smiled at her. "I wasn't sure if it would work out, but it looks like the menus are pretty easy to read."

"And thorough. I'm sure we're going to get many new orders from these." She patted Ally's shoulder.

"I hope so. I was thinking of maybe opening a little ice cream section in the shop. Everyone seems to want ice cream in the summer. Plus we could crush up some chocolates to use as toppings. What do you think?"

Charlotte tilted her head back and forth as she considered the idea. "Well, to be honest, dear, I always thought chocolate and baked goods were enough. Ice cream is a difficult game to get into. First the freezers, then maintaining supply and lastly what to do with oversupply. It gets to be a pain."

"You may be right about that." Ally tapped her chin. "I hadn't really thought that far ahead."

"You have some great ideas as always, Ally, but I think right now we need to keep it simple.

It's a bit of an adjustment for both of us."

"Yes, it is. I'm all alone in that cottage with a pig and a cat." Ally grinned.

"Oh, poor you." Charlotte lofted her eyebrows. "I'm sure that Luke wouldn't mind keeping you company."

"Mee-Maw! I'm not talking about Luke!"

"Why not?" Luke leaned against the side of the booth and looked right into Ally's eyes with a slow, sly smile. "Am I interrupting?"

Ally turned away to hide the deep flush in her cheeks. She pretended to sort through the cookies. "No, of course not, just getting ready for the market to open."

"Do you need any help with anything?" He caught a bag of cookies that almost slid off the edge of the front of the booth. "Here you go." Ally smiled as she took the bag from him. The subtle brush of her fingertips against his skin made her cheeks even hotter.

"I think we have it under control. What are

you doing here?"

"I thought I'd come out and show my support. Plus, I want to get some fresh eggs. I can't stay long, though, I'm on duty as of eleven."

"Well please, have some cookies." Ally held out a bag to him.

"How much?" He pulled out his wallet.

"Oh, no charge for you, Luke." Charlotte patted his hand.

"I insist." He opened his wallet. "I know half of the funds today are going to charity, so please allow me to make my donation." He smiled at Charlotte. His polite nature always impressed her.

"All right, I'll allow it, just this once." Charlotte took the payment and retrieved a few bills from the portable cash register for his change.

"Thanks. I hear Freely Lakes is hosting a party next week." He looked over at Ally, then back to Charlotte.

"Yes, it's a dance. It's going to be fantastic. I'm

on the decorating committee!" Charlotte leaned against the front of the booth. "There is so much to do. We're going to make sure it is quite an event."

"Then I'm sure it will be fantastic. Dare I ask, is there any special gentleman that will be joining you?" He leaned a bit closer to her and curved his lips into a half-smile. Ally watched the way he charmed her grandmother. She loved the way he interacted with her. When they had first met he was very closed off, but now he was starting to come out of his shell. The more she saw him, the more she got to know him, the harder it became to ignore the flutter of her heart whenever he was near.

"Oh, there might be." Charlotte fluttered her lashes in return. "You'll have to attend to find out."

"I'd be more than happy to. Maybe you could convince your granddaughter to invite me?" He glanced over at Ally. Ally froze at the question. She didn't expect it, and her panicked mind tried to come up with a casual response.

"I think I'll be too busy to go." Ally shook her head. "Inventory, and preparing for the big sale next week, and…"

"Nonsense." Charlotte locked eyes with Ally. "Life isn't worth living if you don't take the time to enjoy it, Ally. Besides, how could you turn down this handsome face?" Ally looked back at Luke. Luke widened his eyes and stuck out his bottom lip.

A giggle bubbled up out of Ally as she took in his pout. "How could anyone resist that face?" She shook her head.

"So, it's a date?" Luke asked.

"I'll think about it." Ally grinned and leaned forward to straighten a few more cookies. Luke leaned forward at the same moment in an attempt to catch them before they fell. His lips awkwardly brushed across the rise of her cheek just as she turned towards him to thank him. The near-kiss caused her to stumble back. Luke opened his mouth to speak, but his cell phone rang before he could.

"Oops, I have to check this." He looked at the phone and frowned. "Sorry, I have to go. There's trouble with the traffic from everyone trying to get here to buy up all of these amazing cookies."

"I'm sure that's it." Ally laughed and rolled her eyes.

"He could be telling the truth, Ally, look." Charlotte looked towards the long line that began to form.

"Bye Luke." Ally waved to him.

"You said you'd think about it, remember!" He waved back as he jogged off towards the parking lot. Ally was flustered, but a rush of customers drew her attention. With each package of cookies that she sold she tried to look into the eyes of the customer and express her gratitude. It was a recommended practice in a business management book she'd started to read. According to the book it helped the customer to remember the shop by engaging the pleasure center of their brain. Whether it was true or not

Ally didn't know, but she was happy to try it out. It was also a great way to get to know the new people she saw. Since the farm was in the next town over there were several people that she'd never seen before.

"Can I get three bags?" A man held out a twenty dollar bill.

"Sure. Would you like to try a sample?" Ally offered him a plate of small cookies.

"No thanks. I already know that if they come from Charlotte's shop they're fantastic."

"Well, thank you for that vote of confidence!" Ally smiled and Charlotte waved to him.

"Hi Doc, enjoy the cookies."

"Doc?" Ally glanced over at Charlotte as the man walked away.

"He's a pediatrician."

"Oh, I see." Ally turned back to the next customer in line. When she met his eyes she thought he looked a little familiar, but couldn't place where she knew him from.

"One bag of cookies, please." He glanced down the corridor of booths as if he was looking for someone.

"Sure, here you go." Ally handed him the package. "Don't forget to look over the menu on the back."

"Hey, do you know where I can buy some eggs around here?"

"Sure. Tyler has his own booth near the end, he's selling eggs straight from his barn."

"Great." He nodded and started to walk away.

"Wait, just a moment. I'm sorry, you seem so familiar to me. Do I know you from somewhere?" Ally asked.

He turned back and smiled at her. "I'm surprised that you remembered."

Ally winced. The truth was she didn't actually remember. "It was so long ago."

"Yes. I think you almost broke my leg."

"That's right!" Ally smiled widely. "When the towns did a joint musical production we worked

11

behind the scenes, now I remember. You tripped over a speaker I had left out by mistake. Colin, right?"

"Yes. It's good to see you again, Ally." He nodded to her before walking off. Another customer walked up a few moments after him.

"Can I get a bag of cookies?"

"Sure, coming right up." Ally handed it over to him. She noticed that he snatched the cookies rather roughly from her hand. "That's three dollars, please."

"Three?" He raised an eyebrow. "That's a little high don't you think?"

"Not for these cookies, they are amazing. Would you like to try a sample?"

"No, no thank you." He shook his head and handed over three dollars. Then he briskly walked away and Ally served the next customer.

After the rush Charlotte brushed her hands off on her apron and smiled at Ally.

"I'm going to take Arnold for that walk now. I

want to see what other things are for sale. I'll pick up those eggs for Luke, too."

"Thanks Mee-Maw, I'm sure he'll appreciate that." Ally straightened the packages of cookies that remained. "I'll get Arnold's food ready, he must be starving."

"Good idea. Let's go, Arnold. We'll get you a little work out before we fatten you up." Charlotte snapped a leash onto Arnold's collar and began to lead him away from the booth. The aisles between the booths were populated by people from both towns. Many Charlotte recognized, but some she didn't. There was a time when she knew every face she saw in town. She knew them not just from running the shop, but from her morning and evening walks, her participation in local events, and her desire to be part of a close-knit community.

Overtime things had changed in ways that she didn't really expect. While the small shops still existed there were many larger stores to compete with. The farms in both counties had also begun to disappear. She knew of one at least that had been turned into a golf course to cater to a growing bedroom community that commuted for work and wanted to play at home. As she neared the egg booth she heard a few people chatting about the cookies they had purchased from her booth.

"These are so good. I don't know how she makes them taste so amazing."

"Well, you know they're Charlotte's secret recipes. I wouldn't be surprised if she doesn't even share them with her own granddaughter." Charlotte ducked her head to hide who she was and tried not to laugh. Little did they know that as a child Ally had helped her to create many of those recipes, and they had worked together to come up with the newest chocolate cookie recipe. Charlotte liked tradition, but she also welcomed innovation. She knew if her shop didn't keep up with the times, it would become as extinct as the dinosaurs. Arnold nosed around in the dirt. Each snort billowed dusty sand into the air.

"Oh boy, you really are getting hungry, aren't you, Arnold? Don't worry, I'll be quick." She paused at the back of the line that led to the booth that sold eggs. To her surprise it was quite long. After a few minutes of no one moving Charlotte tapped the shoulder of one of the people that waited in front of her. "Do you know what's taking so long?"

"The guy that runs the booth isn't there." The man in front of her shrugged. "I'm just going to come back later." He turned and walked away from the remainder of the crowd. Charlotte was surprised that the booth would be left unmanned. She noticed a man in the next booth who she recognized. With a hard tug she guided Arnold over to that booth, which sold freshly picked apples. "Excuse me, Harry, do you know where the owner of this egg booth is?"

"Oh sure, the guy running it ran up to the barn to get more eggs. I'm sure that he'll be back soon."

"Okay." Charlotte held tight onto Arnold's leash as a few children ran up to pet him. "He's very friendly, but he's also very hungry, so watch your fingers."

The kids laughed when Arnold snorted at them. Charlotte enjoyed the revelry of seeing the children play with Arnold. She took a deep breath of the fresh air. The kids ran off when their mothers called.

Arnold found something new to be curious about. He snorted then shoved his nose down into the dirt again. He caught a whiff of something that intrigued him and started to tug hard on his leash. It seemed as if he was trying to break free so that he could hunt down his mystery smell.

"Arnold behave." Charlotte glanced over her shoulder in the direction of her booth. She wondered how Ally was handling the crowd that she saw gathered around the booth. She was tempted to go back and help, but she hoped to grab some eggs first. A few more people that waited in line walked away.

"I'm not waiting this long for anyone's eggs." A burly man in a cowboy hat shook his head as he stalked away from the booth.

"I think I agree." Charlotte started to pull Arnold away from the booth, but Arnold resisted. Arnold was very strong when he wanted to be. Charlotte huffed and gave in. Usually, if Arnold was interested in something, he sniffed it and then left it behind for the next interesting thing. This time however he wasn't giving in and Charlotte's shoulder was a bit sore from all of the tugging. She let him wander forward on the leash towards the front of the booth.

When someone called out and waved to her she was distracted for a moment as she waved back. Arnold whipped the leash right out of her hand and rounded the corner of the booth before Charlotte could stop him. "Oh Arnold, get back here!" She edged forward to grab the leash. When she did Arnold looked up at her with a small piece of egg shell stuck to his snout. He snorted at her. She reached down to pull the piece of shell off his snout. When she did she caught sight of a pair of dirt-caked boots. Her breath caught in her throat as she followed the boots up a long pair of legs, slowly past a chest wound and eventually to the familiar face of a young man. It only took one look at the man's pale face for Charlotte to be certain that he was dead. Still, she rushed forward with the hope that maybe she was wrong. When she pressed her fingertips along the curve of his neck, she felt nothing but cool skin.

"Call the police! Nigel is dead!" Charlotte exclaimed.

The few remaining customers that lingered by the booth scattered. Some were on their phones to call for help. Others tried to put as much distance as possible between them and the booth. Charlotte straightened up and did her best to steer Arnold away from what she presumed would become a crime scene. She knew he had probably already done a lot of damage by snorting around. There were several broken eggs on the ground which made it difficult to get Arnold to obey.

As Charlotte struggled with the leash she noticed an open bag of cookies from the chocolate booth on the shelf inside the egg booth. Before she could think much about it, a police officer brushed past her, followed by another, then an EMT. Charlotte stumbled back out of the way of the approaching men. The paramedic confirmed that the man was dead. One of the police officers crouched down beside the body and began to search for signs of foul play. From the chest wound Charlotte didn't doubt that they would find the evidence. She pulled Arnold away and hurried back towards Ally.

Chapter Two

Ally heard the commotion coming from further down the line of booths. Her heart jumped as she saw police officers and an EMT running in the same direction. She knew that her grandmother and Arnold had wandered the same way. She rounded the booth and started towards the gathering crowd. Before she got more than a few steps away she heard Arnold as he snorted along. Charlotte held tight onto his leash and looked at Ally with wide eyes.

"You won't believe what happened?"

"What is it?" Ally braced herself for the worst.

"Nigel Dean, the kid that was running the egg stand, is dead."

"What?" Ally looked in the direction of the police again.

"Did you know him?"

"Not well. I think I went to school with a cousin of his. I do remember the name though."

"It's not surprising that you do. His family is very well-known in the area. In fact his father, Robert Dean, owns the farm next to this one. I'm not sure why Nigel would be working here instead of on his father's farm."

"Do you know what happened to him?" Ally asked.

"I don't know. But it didn't look like a natural death to me. It looked like he was stabbed with something, but I couldn't see a weapon." Ally gathered Arnold's leash and frowned.

"Wait a minute, Robert Dean. Nigel Dean, is Colin Dean's brother? I just saw him at the stand. He bought cookies." Ally's mouth grew dry. "I can't believe it. No, I can't remember ever meeting Nigel, but poor Colin." She glanced around at the crowd. "I wonder if he's still here."

"I don't know, but I'm pretty sure that they're going to shut down the farmer's market."

"What good will that do? They will be getting rid of all of their potential witnesses and maybe even the murderer." Ally crossed her arms and squinted in the direction of the police officers. "I hope they find out what happened quickly."

"That poor boy." Charlotte shook her head. "I don't think he was even out of his twenties yet."

"How could this happen in the middle of this crowd? Someone must have seen who did it. Someone had to hear something."

"I don't know. When I walked up to the booth there were already several people waiting. Maybe the killer attacked when there was a lull in customer traffic." Charlotte watched the steady stream of people that headed for the exit of the farmer's market. "I can't believe I stood there in line while he was dead behind the booth. When I asked Harry, the man in the booth next to Nigel's, he explained that Nigel was still getting more eggs from the barn. I guess he didn't see him come back."

"It's terrible." Ally pulled out her phone. "I'm going to call Luke and let him know what happened. Maybe he will have some information on it."

As the phone rang Ally saw the gurney with a body bag wheeled in through the entry. Her heart lurched at the thought that Nigel's body would soon be inside. She hung up the phone when Luke didn't answer. The PA system crackled to life.

"We're going to ask everyone to clear the area due to an incident. Please leave your contact information with the officer at the exit."

Ally sighed and turned back to the booth. "I guess we better get all of this packed up."

As Ally began to stack the cookies into boxes Charlotte clucked her tongue. "Our cookies were probably the last thing he ate. He had an open bag in the booth with him."

"Really?" Ally pursed her lips. She tried to recall which customer Nigel might have been. "What did he look like?"

"Just like his older brother. Only he had lighter hair."

There were many customers that morning, but Ally couldn't recall seeing Nigel walk up to the booth. "Maybe someone else bought the cookies. I think I would have remembered seeing someone who looked so similar to Colin if they came to the booth. I remembered Colin after all."

"Well, if he didn't buy the cookies, then maybe it was the killer that left them there." Charlotte's eyes narrowed as they walked back towards their booth. "If that's the case, then we might have seen the killer!"

"I bet I did." Ally thought back through all of the faces she recalled. Of course, none of them struck her as a killer. But that didn't mean they weren't. "Hopefully, they will be able to find a fingerprint or something on the package of cookies that will point to the killer."

"Maybe. But even if they do it doesn't prove that whoever left the cookies was the one who killed Nigel. Someone might have given them to him. Another customer might have left them behind."

"You're right." Ally bit into her bottom lip. "I know one person for sure who bought cookies.

Colin."

Charlotte waited with Peaches and Arnold by the booth while Ally took the boxes of cookies to the area where they could leave their goods and then they could drive right up and someone could help them load them into their car.

After Ally had made three trips she picked up Peaches' carrier and took Arnold's leash from her grandmother. They blended into the stream of people that walked away from the farmer's market. As they were about to reach the parking lot, Ally had to pull Arnold out of the way of a man who was in quite a hurry. She scowled as he almost tripped over Arnold. "Excuse me," Ally said.

"Oh, sorry, sorry." The man tried to continue past. She recognized him as someone that had bought cookies earlier in the day. Ally noticed that he wore a shirt that had an emblem on the back. She wasn't quite sure what it was, but she knew that she had seen it somewhere before. It was a large letter D with a silver crown around it. She watched the man as he pushed past and noticed that the heels of his shoes were covered in egg.

"Look at that, Mee-Maw." She grabbed her grandmother's arm to get her attention. As she did, a police officer directed them both to a table to fill out their information. Ally noticed that the man who had nearly tripped over Arnold, continued without stopping at the table. Was he in such a rush because he wanted to evade the police? She knew there wasn't enough reason to alert the authorities, but the entire encounter left her with an uneasy feeling in the pit of her stomach. She noticed that at the exit to the market he was stopped by a police officer who led him over to another table. Ally entered her information quickly and then walked with her grandmother to the car.

***

Once Ally and Charlotte reached the car Ally got Arnold settled in the backseat and Peaches' cat carrier on the seat next to him. Ally drove the short distance to the pick-up point and loaded the boxes of cookies into the trunk.

"I suppose we can take the cookies back to the shop and continue to sell them there," Charlotte suggested when Ally started the car.

"That's a good idea." Ally nodded. Arnold squealed from the backseat. "But we might need to drop these two off first."

"I have an idea. Why don't you drop me off with the cookies. Then you can take Peaches and Arnold home to feed them. I don't think they've had anything to eat all morning."

"Oh, you're right!" Ally frowned. "And I forgot I was going to buy more pig feed while I was there."

"Don't worry, there's an emergency supply under the sink. That should get him through a few days."

"Okay." Ally smiled. "You always think of everything, Mee-Maw."

"Only because of the many, many times that I have forgotten everything." Charlotte laughed.

Ally parked close to the shop and helped her grandmother unload the cookies. Even though it was just past noon the street was dead. Charlotte put her hands on her hips as she looked up and down the street.

"I guess everyone did their shopping at the farmer's market this morning. I don't imagine that we'll have many customers today."

"Then maybe we should close early?"

"I'll give it a little time. When you get back from tending to the animals we'll decide then."

"Okay." Ally gave her a hug. "See you in a few."

As Ally drove away from the shop she saw her grandmother disappear through the door. As much as she loved working with her every day, she missed living with her. Charlotte on the other hand seemed to adore living in the retirement community of Freely Lakes. Ally reminded herself that the important thing was Charlotte's happiness.

When Ally parked at the cottage she got out and opened Peaches' carrier. Peaches bolted straight for the door. Arnold snorted and huffed as if he might not get out of the car. Ally finally coaxed him out. She unlocked the front door and headed straight for the kitchen to take care of the hungry animals. Once she had fed them she grabbed her keys to drive back to the shop. Before she stepped out the door her cell phone rang. Ally answered right away when she saw it was her grandmother.

"Mee-Maw, I'm on my way now to pick you up." Even though Freely Lakes was close enough to walk to from the shop it was still a bit of a hike.

"Don't bother, I already closed up. It's not worth staying open when I haven't seen a single car or person come by. All of our regulars know that we were supposed to be closed today. I have a friend driving me back to Freely Lakes."

"A friend? What friend?" Ally pressed the phone firmly against her ear.

"Never mind that. Just enjoy your evening. I'll

see you at the shop in the morning. Okay?"

"Sure." Ally frowned. She didn't like the idea of some stranger driving her grandmother home. She had to remind herself that Charlotte was perfectly capable of taking care of herself, and had done just that for many years after Ally moved away. But Ally was so curious that she asked the question again. "So, who is taking you home again?"

"Ally, you might want to be a bit more concerned about who is coming to visit you."

"Huh?" Ally peered out through the kitchen window.

"Luke was here looking for you, I told him that you were at the cottage."

"Oh thanks." Ally laughed. "I'm sure that you didn't encourage him to come visit."

"Everything in life can't be dark and heavy, Ally. Luke is your bright light, let him shine."

"Are you going to embroider that on a pillow?"

"I am not an embroiderer."

"No?"

Charlotte sighed. "All right maybe now and then, only when I'm very bored. But I will never ever knit."

"If you say so, Mee-Maw." Ally laughed. "Can you call me when you get in?"

"If you insist."

"I humbly request," Ally said.

"Sure you do."

Ally could hear the warmth in her grandmother's voice as she hung up the phone. She left her cell phone on the kitchen counter and hurried to her room. She knew that she still smelled like farm. She changed into fresh clothes then tugged a comb through her hair. She was glad that her grandmother had warned her about Luke's visit. When she returned to the living room she was surprised that Luke hadn't arrived yet. She checked her phone to see how long it had been since her grandmother called. When she did she found a text from Luke.

Was on my way over but got a call. Will stop by soon.

Ally was a little disappointed as she put down her phone. But her thoughts soon returned to the death at the farmer's market. She sat down at her computer and began surfing the local news sites to see what had been reported about the death. There were many photos of Robert, Nigel and Colin. The family resemblance was uncanny. The headlines all declared that the mysterious death of a prominent farmer's son had rocked the small community. However, as she read the articles the murder didn't seem so mysterious, at least not who two possible suspects might be. Most of the articles explained that there was a family feud and that there was bad blood between family members especially between Robert and Nigel. Some mentioned the bad blood between Colin and Nigel as well. But none went so far as to explain the reason for the family feud. Ally assumed it must have something to do with why Nigel was working at Tyler's farm.

Ally closed her eyes and recalled her interaction with Colin at the farmer's market. Not for an instant did she suspect that he had ill intentions. When she spoke to him was it possible that Nigel was already dead? A knock on the door disrupted her from her internet search. She stood up and walked towards the door. When she opened the door, Luke greeted her with a smile.

"I hope it's not too late," he said as Arnold rushed over to say hello. Luke awkwardly patted the pig on his head.

"No, not at all. Would you like to come in?" She stepped aside from the door.

"Thank you." He crossed the threshold and closed the door behind him. "I just now got off work, and I wanted to check in with you. Well, the truth is, I wanted to see you."

"I'm glad you came by. Do you want a glass of wine?" She gestured to the couch as she walked past it towards the kitchen. "Are you hungry?"

"A glass of wine would be great. I had dinner on duty. Actually, I got together with a few of the local police for dinner. I hoped maybe they had some luck getting some information about the case." He settled on the couch. Ally paused in the entrance to the kitchen and admired him for a moment. Even though he sat down and pretended to relax, his shoulders were tight and his knees were bent as if he was prepared to jump up. Luke was never off duty.

Ally walked over to him with two glasses of wine and handed him one. "Did they?"

"No. Mainbry is being very territorial. Thanks for this." He took a sip of the wine. "I'm sorry I wasn't able to get to you earlier. Things were pretty hectic today. Are you holding up okay?"

"I think so. The funny thing is that I spoke with Colin Dean today."

"You did?" He sat forward some on the couch. "How did that happen?"

"He bought some cookies from the booth. I remembered him from when we worked on a play together in school. He remembered me, too. It was a nice, short conversation."

"Did you know his brother?"

"No, I don't think I ever met him," Ally said. "From the research..."

"Research?" Luke raised an eyebrow.

"Yes, I just looked at the local news and it looks like there was a feud in the Dean family. So, Colin and Robert look like possible suspects."

"I think that's very likely."

"It makes me uncomfortable to think I could have been so friendly with a murderer."

"We don't know anything for sure yet." Luke leaned back on the couch and looked up at the ceiling. "I wish I could get my hands on this case." He gripped the wine glass a little tighter.

"So do I." Ally smiled.

"Then you could get the inside scoop?"

"Yes. I mean Colin must be a suspect. The news sites seem to think that his family feud would give him a motive. He also had plenty of opportunity. He was probably one of the last people to see Nigel alive."

"I would assume the same. Not only that, but sibling rivalry is often a big risk factor when it comes to murder. If there is bad blood between siblings, the grudge tends to be much worse than with someone who is not a relative." Luke set his glass of wine down on the coffee table and turned on the couch to face her. "But let's not spend all of our time talking about crime. Why don't we talk about you dancing with me?"

Ally looked away from him as a familiar heat rushed through her body. She hadn't expected him to be so direct. "I'm still thinking about it."

He reached out and took her glass of wine. He set it down on the table next to his. Then he took her hand in his.

"Ally, you don't have to hedge around it. If you don't want to, it's fine." He searched her eyes. "I thought maybe this was something we might want to explore. Maybe I have the wrong impression."

She withdrew her hand from his and alternated between a smile and a grimace. "It's not that I don't want to. I'm just a little rusty at all of this." She turned back to look at him and took his hand. "Luke, this is definitely something I want to explore. I don't want to give you the wrong impression. I just don't know if this is the right time. I have a lot on my plate with the shop and Mee-Maw getting settled into Freely Lakes."

"I understand that." He brushed his thumb across the back of her hand. "I'm not trying to rush you. You let me know when you're ready. But just because you might not be ready to explore a relationship, I hope you know that I still value our friendship."

"Thank you, Luke." She smiled at him and felt a sense of relief. Luke always found a way to put her at ease.

"But you know, friends do dance together." He grinned.

"Good point." She laughed.

"In fact, I often dance with my friends."

"Oh? Like the guys at work? Somehow I can't picture that."

"Well uh, after a rough shift, we have to blow off steam sometimes."

Ally laughed and leaned into his shoulder. "I bet. I'd love to see that." She gave his hand a light squeeze. "I'll think about the dance, I promise."

"Well, you'll have to let me know soon. It's on Saturday and I need to get my hair done and buy a new suit."

Ally laughed and without much thought brushed her lips across his cheek in a light kiss. "You always find a way to make me feel better, Luke."

"You just did the same." He stared into her eyes. For just a moment she thought he might lean in to kiss her. Instead he picked up his wine glass, finished the contents and stood up.

"Good night, Ally. Don't stay up all night

investigating."

"Would I do that?" She took the empty glass from him.

"Mmhm." He winked at her and walked towards the door. Ally thought about stopping him and asking him to stay, but the truth was the longer she was alone with him the less she could resist him.

"Good night, Luke."

He smiled at her as he closed the door behind him. Ally finished her wine with thoughts of Luke rolling through her mind. Would she ever be brave enough for there to be a right time?

Chapter Three

In the morning the first streams of sunlight that worked their way through the blinds in Ally's bedroom, woke her right out of a fitful sleep. Her thoughts were filled with the murder, especially who Nigel's murderer might be. As she sat up in her bed Peaches jumped onto the bed beside her.

"I know, I know, you're ready for breakfast." Ally scratched the top of the cat's head and behind her ears. "I promise I will get it for you soon. But, first I need to figure out some things. Nigel is dead, and although the press seems to be portraying that his conflict with his family is the reason, I'm not sure that I agree. What could go wrong between siblings or a father and a son that would lead to such a terrible act?"

Peaches purred and rubbed her cheek against Ally's hand. "I know, not everyone is the same. Some people don't have that close connection with others." She stood up from her bed and began to walk towards the kitchen. Peaches rushed past her, so close that she almost tripped Ally. Ally stumbled and caught herself on the counter in the kitchen. As she regained her balance she caught sight of a shadow approaching the kitchen door. At first she thought that it might be Luke, however the moment that the person knocked Ally knew it was her grandmother.

"Morning, Mee-Maw, I've told you before you don't have to knock!" She shook her head.

"I just think it's polite, dear." She hurried past her with two cups of coffee. "I thought we might both need these today."

"Thank you so much. I am having a hard time getting my mind on anything other than Nigel."

"So am I. I think maybe we need to look into this a bit more."

"Really?" Ally sat down at the table and gestured for her grandmother to join her. "Do you think there's some way we can get more information?" Peaches jumped up into Ally's lap.

"I think we should pay our respects and have

a conversation with Nigel's brother, Colin."

"How are we going to do that?" Ally stroked Peaches' fur. "I'm not sure that we can get a personal invite."

"Oh trust me, I will get us in." Charlotte smiled. "There's always a way in. Especially when you bring chocolates. Besides, you said that Colin remembered you. I doubt he'd be rude enough to turn you away."

"If you think you can get us in, then I would be happy to accompany you. But I don't know if Colin will welcome me. We only knew each other for a couple of weeks years ago, that was all."

"Well, that might just be enough. I want to look Colin in the eyes. I watched the news this morning and the reporter interviewed a few people and they said that they had seen Colin talking to Nigel at the farmer's market. He hasn't been arrested yet, but I think it's just a matter of time," Charlotte said.

"Well, then we'd better get to him before he is."

"They also mentioned that there was no struggle and Nigel's wallet was still on him so robbery is not suspected."

"Interesting. Luke said that the Mainbry police department is not being very forthcoming with information on the case. I doubt they would let us or Luke anywhere near Colin once he is in custody."

"I guess you need to get dressed. It isn't proper to visit people in pajamas." Charlotte smiled.

"Are you sure?" Ally quirked her lips. "I might start a new trend."

"I don't think so," Charlotte said. "But then again, you are always full of surprises."

As Ally walked down the hall to her room to change her grandmother's voice followed after her.

"Did you say yes to the dance yet?"

"I'll be out in a minute!" Ally said trying to avoid the question and change the subject.

She thought she should wear something that would give a more professional impression. What was appropriate attire for visiting a grieving family? She decided on black pants and a light pink blouse. When she returned to the kitchen Charlotte held her purse out to her.

"Let's get going. There are some flowers at the shop so we can pick them up together with some chocolates on the way. I also want to leave enough time to open the shop after."

"Okay." Ally gave Arnold a pat on the head then they headed out to Ally's car.

After picking up the flowers and chocolates from the shop Charlotte mentioned everything that she found out at Freely Lakes as they drove to the farm.

"Apparently everything went sour between Bob and Nigel when Bob married Linda."

"Really?" Ally said.

"Yes, it got so bad between Bob and Nigel that he refused to even let Nigel on the property."

"All over his new wife?"

"Yes, I believe so," Charlotte said.

"Do you know her?" Ally asked.

"She's come into the shop a few times, but I don't really know her. I do know what her favorite chocolates are though."

"You know what all our customers like." Ally smiled.

"Yes, it is a pity it won't help solve a murder."

"Well, Linda seems to have broken up a family."

"According to my sources. Popular belief is that she married Bob just for his money. Apparently, she has already been divorced once from a wealthy, older man."

"Hm." Ally turned down the long road that led to both farms. "Maybe Nigel found some way to prove that. Maybe we should consider the wife a suspect, too."

"I think you might be right about that. From what I understand Nigel told everyone that would listen how he felt about his father's wife. Even if he didn't find any proof, maybe she didn't like how he talked about her. Ally turned onto Bob's driveway. It was long, narrow, and led to a semi-circle parking area. She got out of the car, then helped her grandmother get the flowers and chocolates out.

"Do you think they'll let us in?" Ally asked.

"I made a call while you were changing. I set up a meeting with Colin. He only agreed to it when I mentioned you."

Ally frowned as she looked up at the large home. Her heart fluttered at the thought of having a meeting with a possible murderer.

"Ally." Charlotte rested her palm on the curve of her granddaughter's elbow. "We have to be careful in there. Bob has a lot of influence in the community. Let's just remember to be courteous."

"Okay, I will." Ally smiled at her grandmother. "I'll be on my best behavior I promise."

"Good." Charlotte looked uncharacteristically nervous as she followed Ally towards the house.

Ally paused at the bottom of the steps. Each of the stone railings that lined the steps was topped with intricately carved stone lions. It was a touch of extravagance amidst the rural setting. She brushed a fingertip along the mane of one of the lions.

"Ally? Are you coming?" Charlotte paused in front of the door at the top of the stairs and turned back to look at Ally.

"Aren't these interesting? I would expect something like horses, or even bulls, but lions?"

"It's a symbol of rural royalty. It's tradition around here for the oldest farms to have a lion somewhere in their decor. I guess that Bob decided to have two. That doesn't surprise me, as originally his family owned both this farm and Tyler's farm."

"Wow, that must have been a massive amount of land."

"Yes, and hard to tend. From what I hear it got to be a little out of control, which is why it was portioned off. But then that may not be true. It's second hand information." Charlotte reached up and rang the doorbell. Ally stepped up beside her. After a few seconds the front door opened and Colin greeted them.

"Charlotte, Ally, hello, thanks for coming."

"I'm so sorry for your loss, Colin, we both are," Charlotte said as she handed him the flowers and chocolates.

"Thank you. Let's go through," he said as he led them to a large sitting room.

"I have to say, I don't think it's quite set in. I keep expecting to see Nigel around town. I just..." He cleared his throat. "I just find it very hard to accept."

"Of course you do. It will be hard for a long time, Colin." Charlotte reached out and pressed his hand between both of hers. "Grief is not something that can be rushed."

He nodded as he sat down in a wingback chair. Charlotte and Ally sat on an elegant couch across from him. Ally noticed the fine, gold thread that wound a subtle pattern through the stiff off-white material. She traced a fingertip along it as Colin spoke.

"I understand that. At least I think I do. But this feels different to me. It's more than just the loss. I have to know what happened to him. Who killed him? Why he was killed?" Colin said. "I need justice to be served."

"It will be." The words slipped past Ally's lips before she had time to think them through. She wanted them to be true. "With the police looking into it, I'm sure the crime will be solved in no time."

"I'm not so sure about that." Colin shook his head. "I think the police are eager to sweep this under the rug. They've interrogated me and my father several times, as if he would have anything to do with his own son's death. The truth is that yes, our family was going through a difficult time, but all families do at some point."

"Sometimes it helps the heart to talk about it, Colin." Charlotte met his eyes. "I want you to know that we are here for you. The loss of a family member can make you feel very isolated from the rest of the world. I hope that you and your father are able to support each other at this time."

"We're trying." Colin reached up and rubbed the back of his neck. "You see, my little brother, Nigel, didn't have the kind of upbringing that I did. My mother was a big part of my childhood, and unfortunately she passed away before Nigel could benefit from her warmth and wisdom. I tried to spend as much time with him as I could, but he was often left to his own devices, as my father and I worked the farm. He became less and less connected with the family business. For some reason he got it in his head that my father was the one that was on the wrong side of the fight over the land. He turned against the family, in favor of Tyler, and that was not easy for my father or me to take. So yes, there has been some frustration on both sides. But that didn't stop us from being a family. We always had a strong family bond. You understand?" He looked between the two of them. "Of course you do. Family doesn't break that easily."

"No, it doesn't." Charlotte smiled softly. "Family is much stronger than that."

"And your stepmother?" Ally prompted and met Colin's eyes.

"Who?" Colin narrowed his eyes then nodded. "Oh, Linda, right. I'm sorry I don't think of her with that title."

"Is there a reason for that?" Charlotte's tone was gentle, but she leaned forward some.

"Well, I was an adult when they married. It's not as if she's in any kind of mother role. She's only five years older than I am." He raised an eyebrow as he looked at Ally. "It's a little shocking to be honest. I didn't blame Nigel for being upset. But I thought he would get over it. You know, it was my father's decision, and his life. So why should we care what he does? But Nigel didn't see it that way. He took it as a personal insult for some reason. They did not get along."

"What about the way Linda treated Nigel? Was she kind to him?" Ally asked.

"No, not at all. She came on a little strong when she married our father. She wanted to be taken seriously as a member of the family. But she hadn't really done anything to earn that place. We were both wary of how long she would actually be part of the family. Nigel was a bit more vocal about his misgivings and of course she took offense to that."

Ally tapped her fingertips on the curve of her knee. "So, she had some animosity towards Nigel."

"Yes, but that doesn't mean anything." He shook his head. "I keep trying to explain, every family has its problems. But Nigel wasn't killed because of them."

"Then why do you think he was, Colin?" Charlotte looked into his eyes. "You knew your brother well. Why would someone have gone after him like this?"

Colin tightened his lips. He looked down at his hands for some time. "Couldn't it have been some random person?"

"Sure, it could have." Ally drew his attention back to her. "However, from what I understand they don't believe that is the situation as in cases like that, there usually is a pretty clear motive. Such as robbery, or a very visible fight. Your brother still had his wallet on him with all of its contents, and there was no sign of a struggle."

"How do you know that?" he asked with wide eyes.

"It was on the news," Ally said.

"I see." He sighed. "And yes I already know that no one saw what happened to him. So I guess there's not much to go on."

"No, it doesn't seem like there is," Ally said.

"I am probably their number one target. I mean who can blame them. The way our relationship has been portrayed and of course I was there."

"Out of curiosity, where were your father and stepmother?" Ally leaned forward slightly.

"They were both on a tour of a neighboring farm. It's the one behind Tyler's. My father has been wanting to purchase it, and he thought this year's crop would put him in the position to be able to. But now that's changed."

"Why is that?" Ally asked.

"One of our largest crops has failed for some reason. We're still investigating why. So there may not be enough money. They decided to go on the tour anyway. I took advantage of the opportunity to speak to Nigel. Now that makes me the main suspect. That's why I agreed to meet with you this morning."

Ally's eyes widened. "Why did you agree?"

Colin sighed and rested his hands on the tops of his knees as he looked at them. "I know you were both there when, what happened, happened. I thought maybe you saw something, or heard something that might help me figure out all of this. I don't trust the police to find his murderer when they seem so focused on me and my father, so I'm trying to look into things on my own." He looked towards Charlotte. "You found my brother, didn't you?"

"Yes, I did." Charlotte glanced over at Ally, then back to Colin. "But I'm sorry, I have no idea who hurt your brother."

"Maybe you know more than you think you do. If you think about it." He folded his hands together and sat forward. "Sometimes a person can hear or see something that doesn't seem important. But it might be to me."

"All I know is that the vendor in the booth next to his said he saw Nigel go back to the barn for eggs, and that he would be back soon," Charlotte said.

"Well, he was obviously mistaken." Colin raised an eyebrow. "Unless he is lying."

"I assumed that he just didn't see Nigel come back." Charlotte shrugged.

"That's right, the police mentioned that he said he didn't see anything at all. I wonder how that's possible? Nigel's body was on the ground for how long?" Colin asked.

"Try not to think about it too much, dear." Charlotte clucked her tongue lightly. "Nothing good comes of concentrating on these things."

"But if I don't, who will?" Colin shook his head. "I feel like I'm in a race against time. The police seem to be concentrating on pinning this on me or my father, or both of us, and they're not going to rest until they are able to do that."

"Colin, I'm sure they'll discover the truth, but there's no harm in speeding up the process and making sure that they do. If you tell me everything that you know, I'll see if I can help you," Ally said. "If you want me to help, Colin, I will." Ally couldn't bear to think of an innocent man going to jail and a murderer roaming free. She didn't know how she could help, but she wanted to try.

"Ally." Charlotte stole a glance over at her, but Ally remained fixated on Colin.

"You would do that?" Colin stared back at her. "Why?"

"Because I know what it's like to be suspected of a murder you didn't commit. I also know what it's like to lose someone before their time, Colin. I know how devastating it can be. Someone should pay for what they did to Nigel. The right person." Ally neglected to mention that she also enjoyed a little sleuthing.

"All right." He shrugged. "What could it hurt? I already told you everything I could think of, but if there's something else you want to know, feel free to ask."

"There's one thing." Ally tapped the screen of her phone.

"What is it?" Colin asked.

"Well, people saw you there, talking with your brother. It wasn't long before he was murdered."

"Oh, so you think I did it, too?" Colin narrowed his eyes and looked away from her with a sharp tilt of his chin.

"No, that's not what I'm saying, Colin. I'd like to know what you were talking to him about. If I can get an idea of his frame of mind, it might help."

"Okay." Colin glanced towards the door of the study, then looked back towards her. "I went there to speak to Nigel. I knew he would be there, and I knew that my father wouldn't be, so I went to the farmer's market to speak to him."

"Did you argue?" Ally studied him.

"No. Not exactly. He wasn't happy to see me, but he was willing to talk. I wanted to mend things with him, and bring him back into the family. He actually listened." He cringed and shook his head. "I know this will be hard to believe, but Nigel told me that he had something very important to tell me. But he wanted to speak to both me and my father about it at the same time. From his tone, I knew it was something bad. I tried to get him to tell me, but then the booth got busy. I decided to leave to get my father. I thought maybe he would be willing to talk to Nigel if he knew that it was important. I drove over to the neighboring farm where my father was meant to be. By the time I came back Nigel was gone."

"Did you come back with your father? Did you speak to him at the other farm?" Ally pressed.

"No, I didn't. I couldn't find him. When I called him he said that he and Linda had finished the tour and went to a nearby coffee shop. I mentioned what Nigel had said, and he blew up at me. He said he would never speak to Nigel again and that I shouldn't either." He swallowed hard.

"Sounds like he was pretty worked up." Charlotte frowned.

"Yes, he was." Colin nodded. "So was I to be honest. When I got back to the farmer's market the police were already arriving. I didn't realize why until I got to the booth."

"Did you speak to the police then?" Ally asked.

"No, I didn't. I couldn't get near Nigel, and I guess I was afraid of being accused. So I took off. Maybe that was a mistake."

"Maybe, but maybe it was a good thing." Ally met his eyes. "If you had spoken to them they might have arrested you on the spot. I think you need to be careful about what you say and to whom," Ally suggested. She had learnt this firsthand when she had been suspected of murder.

"I realize that now. I don't think it will matter what I do or say though, the police have me in their sights and they're not going to give up until I'm in handcuffs. I've never been arrested in my life. I'll admit, I'm scared."

"I don't blame you for being afraid, Colin. I'll see if I can find out anything for you and see if I can help you," Ally said.

"Thank you. That's good." He stood up and offered his hand. "You have no idea how good it feels to have someone on my side. I feel like the whole town is pointing its finger at me."

Ally shook his hand and then released it with an encouraging smile. "Try not to get too caught up in that. I think you should contact a lawyer in case. I'm sure this will all get straightened out."

"Thanks for your time, Colin." Charlotte offered her hand to him. "And again, I'm sorry for your loss. Remember that even though all of this is happening, you will still need time to grieve."

"Thank you for that, Charlotte. I feel like I can't begin to accept my brother's death with all of this hanging over my head."

As Colin walked the two to the front door, Ally noticed a man standing in the long hallway that led to another section of the house. He didn't speak a word to either of them. Ally looked quickly away. Colin didn't seem to notice him. Once Charlotte and Ally were through the door Colin began to close it. Before he got it shut all the way Ally heard a raised voice.

"How could you have done this? How? Am I just supposed to accept this from you, Colin?"

The shout was so loud that it caused Charlotte and Ally to freeze at the bottom of the steps. Colin pushed the door closed.

"Who is yelling?" Charlotte frowned.

"I think it was his father, Bob. I saw him in the hallway when we were leaving."

"Do you think we should check on Colin?" Charlotte asked.

"I'm not sure if we should interfere and they are both quiet now, but did you hear what he said? Was he asking Colin how he could have killed his brother?"

Charlotte sighed as they walked towards the car. "I hope not. If that's the case then we might have just taken the wrong side."

"I'm not sure that I've taken a side. But it's hard for me to believe that Colin would be angry enough to hurt his brother."

"It's hard for me to believe, too. However, Bob on the other hand." Charlotte tilted her head towards the front door of his house as she opened the door to Ally's car. "I think he might be hot headed enough to kill anyone if they crossed him."

"That's a good point." Ally climbed into the

car and started the engine. "He wasn't far from the farmer's market either."

"No, he wasn't. And when Colin went looking for him he wasn't at the farm."

"He claimed to be at a nearby coffee shop." Ally drove down the long driveway. "Well, it can't be too far from here. Maybe we should see if we can find it."

"I think that's a good idea. We could use the coffee before we open the shop."

"Here, do a search on my phone to see if there are any coffee shops listed nearby." Ally handed her the phone. Charlotte looked at it for a moment. Then she began jabbing the letters on the screen.

"I don't know how to do this." She sighed with frustration.

"That's okay." Ally pulled the car over and showed her grandmother what to do. "Looks like there's one two miles down the road." Ally checked her phone to see if there were any other nearby coffee shops. When she did she saw that the next closest one was over ten miles away. "The one only two miles away has to be it. It's not far at all." Ally smiled and pulled out onto the road.

Chapter Four

Within minutes Ally and Charlotte were at the coffee shop. She and her grandmother walked up to the shop. It was a small place with only a few tables and a long coffee bar. The woman behind the counter was young with a bright smile and wore her red hair in a tight braid.

"Morning. Welcome to Mainbry Café, would you like to try our flavor of the month?"

"Just two regular coffees, please." Charlotte glanced at Ally. "Why don't you find us a seat?"

Ally nodded and walked over to one of the small tables. While her grandmother chatted with the waitress she placed a call to Luke.

"Hi Ally, how are you?"

"I'm hoping that you won't be upset with me."

"Why would I be upset?" He paused. "Wait, I'm not sure that I want to know."

"It's not too big of a deal. I met with Colin

Dean this morning."

"Oh? From what I've heard he might be arrested soon for his brother's murder."

"Are you sure?"

"Well, you know how Mainbry is being, I can't be absolutely certain, but that's the rumor. Why would I be upset with you about that?"

"Because I might have told Colin that I'm going to see if I can help him find out who the murderer is." Ally cringed, she knew that Luke would not like her investigating, but she hoped he might help if he knew the truth.

"What?" Luke's voice raised an octave. "Why would you tell him that?"

"Because I believe he's innocent and I know what it is like to be suspected of committing murder when you are innocent."

"I don't think you should get involved, Ally. Not that it proves anything, but Colin's fingerprints were on the bag of cookies found in the egg booth. Not to mention the family feud being his motive and the fact that he was at the market. Colin looks very guilty from a police point of view."

"I know he does. But you weren't there with me today, Luke. I don't think he did this. I think he's a broken-hearted brother who might be arrested for his brother's murder and I have to try and help him."

"Ally, please be careful."

"Yes, I will be." Ally glanced over at her grandmother. She had the coffees in her hands, but had not stopped her conversation with the waitress.

"Ally, Colin has a lot against him. Sibling rivalry can be vicious," Luke said.

"I think that maybe there was no sibling rivalry. At least that's what Colin claims. He said he was there to apologize to his brother, and to draw him back into the family business. He made it seem as if he was a protective big brother to a wayward young man. In fact, he even asked if we noticed anything at the market that could help with the investigation. He seemed relieved when I said that I would see what I could find out."

"Really?" Luke cleared his throat. "That doesn't sound like someone who feels guilty. But it also sounds like it might be a cunning plan to throw suspicion off him."

"Maybe it is," Ally said thoughtfully. "Murderers can be quite clever and calculating, but that doesn't seem to be the case here."

"Why do you think that?" Luke asked.

"If the person who did this was clever, then why was the murder so sloppy? Why kill Nigel right there, with so many people around? The risk of being caught had to be huge. So why would anyone take that risk?"

"Yes, it does seem rather impulsive of the killer. It feels a bit like a crime of passion. Which again puts Colin in the spotlight. Or even his father or stepmother. Unless...did Nigel have a girlfriend?"

"Not that Colin mentioned. But they had been

estranged for some time. Maybe there was someone new in Nigel's life that Colin didn't know about."

"Ask his co-workers. That's the best way to find out anything about anyone."

"Oh really?" Ally asked. "Is that the best way to find out things about you?"

"No." He paused in such a way that made Ally think he smiled. "The best way is just to ask me."

"I don't know, you strike me as the strong, silent type."

"I've learned that saying too much can get me in trouble."

"Well, I'd like to know a lot more about you."

"I want to know more about you, too. Like, if you're going to step on my toes when we dance."

"Oh, you think you're pretty clever don't you?" Ally laughed.

"I would like to tell you to stay out of this, but seeing as we both know that's not going to happen, just promise me you'll be cautious with all of this. If there's any chance of Colin being the killer he could turn on you very quickly."

"I'm being careful. I promise. Oh, I have to go, Luke. Let me know if you find out anything new, please."

"I will try."

Ally hung up the phone just as her grandmother walked up with the coffees. She sat down across the table from Ally.

"Who was that?" She set a coffee in front of Ally.

"Thanks for the coffee, Mee-Maw. It was Luke."

"Anything new?"

"Just that he's not happy that I'm sticking my nose in this and Colin might be arrested sometime soon."

"Well, I have something to tell you." Charlotte leaned across the table and lowered her voice. "Bob is a liar."

"Oh?"

"Yes, I asked the young woman at the counter if she remembered who was in here yesterday. I didn't even get to describe Bob and his wife before she stopped me. She said they were closed because they decided to run a booth of specialty coffees at the farmer's market. They knew that their regular customers would be at the market. So, if the shop didn't open, then how did Bob and his wife have a coffee here?"

"Oh, that is a very good question. I doubt they would have driven much further just for coffee. So, if they lied, why did they lie?"

"To cover up for the fact that Colin couldn't find them at the farm they claimed to visit. His father had to come up with something fast. He probably didn't know the coffee shop was closed." Charlotte sipped her coffee. "I'm more suspicious of Bob than Colin."

"That may be the case. Especially if that was him today that we heard lose their temper," Ally said.

Charlotte clucked her tongue and added some

sugar to her coffee. As she stirred the liquid with a long, thin, red stick Ally's mind drifted. She thought back to the day before and all the people she had seen at the farmer's market. As she sorted through her memories of the faces that she saw in search of Bob's, she recalled one particular man that had left quite an impression.

"Wait a minute!" Ally looked across the table at her grandmother. "I don't know if Bob was there, but I do remember something interesting."

"What's that?"

"That guy that almost tripped on Arnold. He was wearing a shirt with the Dean family farm emblem on the back of it!"

"Oh." Her grandmother nodded. "Yes, now I remember. It must have been one of Bob's employees."

"I think he was and he bought cookies that morning."

"I don't remember that," Charlotte said.

"But why would one of Bob's employees have

been at the farmer's market, on Tyler's property? I am sure, that if Bob didn't want his sons involved with Tyler, then he would not want his employees involved with him either."

"He probably wouldn't," Charlotte said.

"I wonder if I could get some information about him from Colin."

"Maybe he'll also know if Nigel had a girlfriend."

"Don't you think if he had a girlfriend she would have come forward by now?" Ally said.

"Well, she might have seen the police, we don't know. Also, if she was someone new in Nigel's life, she might not have ever met his family. He may have told her horrible things about his family, too. We can't know what."

"Of course, Nigel may have been single, too."

"True, but something tells me he wasn't. I noticed the way his hair was trimmed and his fingernails were clean. A man who works on a farm doesn't always worry about those types of things."

"That's a very good point, Mee-Maw. I'm surprised you were able to see that. You're so observant."

"I learned all of my detective skills from you, my love."

"Hm. Mee-Maw, are you trying to butter me up?"

"Maybe." She lifted an eyebrow. "Are you going to go with Luke to the dance?"

"Oh, I don't know. I don't really have anything to wear, and it seems a little high school, don't you think?"

"What's wrong with that?" Charlotte shrugged. "Trust me when you get to be my age you're going to wish you were back in high school, even with all the drama."

"Maybe." Ally frowned. "I'm just not sure that I'm ready for it."

"Ready for what? Dancing?"

"Please Mee-Maw, you know how intimate

dancing can be. I can barely look at him without blushing, how am I supposed to hold it together with his arms around me?"

"You're not." She smiled. "That's the point. You're supposed to let it flow."

"And that's what I'm not ready for." Ally winked.

"What is holding you back, Ally? Are you afraid he will hurt you?" Ally froze at the question. Her grandmother could be quite blunt when she wanted to be.

"I'm not sure that's it. Sometimes I worry I might hurt him. I just think the whole idea of a relationship, there's just so much pressure around that. I really enjoy Luke being part of my life."

"Ah." Charlotte took her hand with a subtle press to the back of it. "You're worried that if things go wrong you'll lose him."

Ally stared into her eyes. "Is it that obvious?"

"Only to those with experience in these

things. But that settles it," Charlotte said.

"Settles what?"

"You're in love."

"Wait a minute, Mee-Maw, we haven't even had a date yet." Ally laughed.

"No, you haven't. But he's still important enough to you that you will do everything you can to protect his place in your life."

"Because we're friends."

"If you say so." Charlotte offered a wistful smile. "When you're young, Ally, you always think you have forever. But love doesn't always wait."

"Please, stop talking about love." Ally shook her head. "But I understand what you're saying. It feels like I'm standing at the edge of a waterfall, fighting the current."

"Mmhm." Charlotte met her eyes. "And when you give up the fight, when you let go and crash over the edge, I promise you, it will be the most glorious experience of your life."

"What if it's not?" Ally bit into her bottom lip.

"That isn't as important as the possibility that it might be. Would you really trade the chance at an experience like that for a permanent battle with the current?" She tapped the back of Ally's hand. "One day you won't have a choice anymore. Either the water will run dry, or your knees will buckle."

"Maybe. But it's not today."

"Maybe not," Charlotte agreed.

"With Luke's job he's always getting called away. It feels like we have this deep connection, but we don't actually know much about each other. Our likes and dislikes, our pasts, our hopes for the future."

"Oh, I like that you're thinking about the future." Charlotte grinned.

"You know it wasn't that long ago that you weren't so sure about Luke."

"I think he's proven on more than one occasion that he can be trusted. Of course I'll have to do a more thorough investigation before things get too serious."

"I imagine he'd love that." Ally laughed.

"I'm serious though, Ally. This is a nice time for you and Luke. You may think you're still fighting, but you're already going over the edge. Take some time to really get to know him. You won't get this time back."

"Thanks for the advice, Mee-Maw." Ally smiled. "I'll call now to see if Colin knows if Nigel had a girlfriend and to ask him about the man from the Dean farm that was at the market." Ally dialed Colin's number and waited for him to answer. She pushed her fingertips along her coffee cup and twirled it.

"Ally?"

"Colin, I have a couple of quick questions. Do you know someone who works on your farm that might have gone to the market yesterday?"

"I don't think any of them would risk being seen on Tyler's land. Oh wait, except for Zac of course."

"Zac?"

"Yes. He and Nigel were close friends. Even though Nigel left the farm I think Zac's been to see him a few times. I can't think of anyone else who would have been out there."

"Was there any bad blood between Zac and Nigel?"

"No, they were good friends. Nigel even made me make sure that my father let Zac take over his position when he left. Better pay than what Zac would have been making."

"Okay, thanks for the information, Colin," Ally said. "I also wanted to check if you know whether Nigel had a girlfriend. Was there anyone special that he was seeing?"

"Actually yes, I think he did," he said. "I heard on the grapevine that he recently started seeing a girl that works in town."

"Do you know her name?"

"Tracy I think. Tracy Flowers. Yes, that's it. I remember because she works in a flower shop.

What are the chances of that?"

"Pretty slim," Ally said. "Thanks for the information, Colin."

"Thank you, Ally."

He hung up the phone. Ally looked across the table at her grandmother.

"Apparently Colin heard that Nigel had been seeing Tracy Flowers, a girl that works at the flower shop."

"Wow, what a name." Charlotte smiled.

"Do you think you could open up the shop today?" Ally asked.

"Of course I can." Charlotte chuckled.

"Great. Then I'm going to head out to meet with Zac."

"Who is Zac?"

"He's a farmhand that works on Bob's farm. Colin said that Zac and Nigel had gotten quite close when they worked together."

"Let's get going, I don't want to open the shop

late," Charlotte said.

"Thanks for opening the shop for me." The feet of Ally's chair scraped across the floor as she stood up. "I'll drop you at the shop and let you know if I find out anything from Zac or Tracy."

"Perfect." Charlotte picked up her coffee cup and followed Ally out to the car.

Chapter Five

After Ally dropped her grandmother off at the shop she drove back in the direction of Bob's farm. A part of her hoped she'd catch Bob alone so she could casually mention that the coffee shop was closed on the day he claimed to be there and see what his response was. However, her first interest was Zac.

As she pieced together the events of the day she recalled the person who she now thought was Zac purchasing a bag of cookies. She wondered if it was possible that he had an argument with Nigel that ended up in murder. That would explain why he was in such a hurry to avoid the police that he almost tripped over Arnold. However, if Nigel had been kind enough to ensure that Zac got a raise and a promotion when he left why would Zac have killed him?

Instead of turning down the main drive that led to the Dean house Ally turned down the next side road that led to the barn. Before she parked she noticed the man who had bought cookies, who she presumed was Zac, near the barn. As she parked he disappeared into the barn. She stepped out of the car and glanced around. Colin might be okay with her being there, but he was not the one who owned the farm. His father was. She doubted that Bob would be too pleased to find her there. She lingered a few moments beside her car in the hopes that Zac would make his way back out of the barn.

When that time had passed Ally knew she had to make a move. She walked up to the barn and peeked inside. Zac wasn't hard to spot as he tossed bales of hay from one section of the barn to another. It was an act that Ally could see no real purpose for, but she wasn't too familiar with good farming practices and Zac was focused on it. She cleared her throat. Zac turned around to face her with a half-open mouth.

"What are you doing here?"

"Hi there. Zac right?" Ally leaned against the open door of the barn. "Sorry to bother you in the middle of work." Zac brushed his gloves against the dirty legs of his jeans.

"What is it that you want?"

"We met yesterday, didn't we? Oh right, I wouldn't exactly say we met. My name is Ally."

"Okay Ally, but what do you want?"

"I know that you and Nigel were very good friends. At least that's what I've heard. Is that true?"

"Yes." Zac gazed off for a moment and then looked back at Ally. "Since he left the family farm we hadn't seen each other as much. But we got together now and then."

"I was wondering if you might know of anyone that had anything against him."

"Uh, yeah, his brother, and his dad. Just like I told the detective investigating the case." He brushed his hair back from his eyes. "I can't believe they went this far."

"So, you think that his family was involved in his death?"

"Of course. I saw Nigel and Colin arguing less than half an hour before Nigel was killed. Who else would kill him?" He narrowed his eyes. "I've seen some cruel people in my life, but to kill your own brother, now that's really low."

Ally cringed. She was sure that if Zac spoke to the detective that way that would only make their suspicions of Colin stronger. Colin was right, he did need all of the help that he could get. Unless she was completely wrong and she was actually helping a murderer.

"What about a girlfriend?" Ally took out her phone. "Was there anyone special that Nigel was seeing?" Ally hoped he would confirm that he had been seeing Tracy or maybe even let her know if there was someone else that Colin didn't know about.

"No, no one that I know about." He shrugged. Maybe the rumors Colin had heard about Tracy had been wrong.

"How had Nigel been acting lately? Was he real angry about anything?"

"Not really. I mean, he hated his dad. He talked about that a lot."

"And Colin?"

Zac shrugged. "That was different. Actually, I think Nigel was more upset about him."

"Upset how?" Ally looked at him intently.

"He was close to Colin I guess." Zac balled his hands into fists. "It's terrible that his brother would turn against him like this."

"Yes, it is." Ally sighed as she tried to keep him on her side in case she needed more information from him. "I guess people just don't understand what real loyalty is anymore."

"Yeah, I guess not." He cleared his throat. "Anyway, I've got to get back to work."

"Sure. Thanks for your time, Zac." Zac adjusted his hat and walked away from Ally and the barn. Before he got too far she called out to him. "Zac, are there chickens you tend here?"

"Chickens?" He nodded his head. "Yes, chickens and dairy."

Ally looked down at his shoes and noticed that they were very clean with only a little bit of dirt on them. Obviously Zac had cleaned off the egg from the day before. She watched as he disappeared into one of the fields. She scanned the fields and noticed that there were several patches of dead crops. As Colin had claimed the farm appeared to be in trouble. Ally glanced at the time on her phone. She hadn't spent long with Zac. Instead of going straight to the shop she decided to visit the flower store in Mainbry. She might just get lucky and find Tracy Flowers behind the counter.

**

The main street in Mainbry was a lot busier than it had been the day before. It took Ally some time to find a spot, but once she did she noticed that most of the foot traffic was headed for the convenience store at the end of the block. She assumed the owner was having a sale. When she stepped into the flower store she was greeted by an assortment of alluring fragrances. Behind the counter a woman arranged flowers into a small glass vase.

"Tracy?" She paused in front of the counter. Tracy smiled as she looked back at Ally.

"So says the name tag!" She pointed at the bright yellow flower pinned to her shirt. "Are you interested in an arrangement?"

"Not today actually. I wonder if I could speak to you for a moment."

Tracy glanced around the shop. Ally was the only other person there. "Sure, we're not busy."

"Did you know Nigel Dean?"

"Oh." Tracy's smile faded. "Yes, I knew him."

"I've heard that you two were dating."

"We saw each other a few times. But, he didn't seem very interested. At least not until a few days ago."

"A few days ago? What happened then?"

"He started calling me all the time. He was asking me all kinds of questions, like he was interested in my work."

"That sounds nice."

"It was in a way, but it was also kind of weird, because you know I just work here for a paycheck, it's not like I grow the flowers myself. The owner does that."

"Oh, I see. Did you talk to him the morning he died?"

"No, I didn't. Actually, the night before I told him I wanted to go out. He gave me this lame excuse about having to do something alone. I've dated enough guys to know when I'm getting blown off. But I liked Nigel, so I thought I'd see what he was up to."

"You followed him?"

"Just long enough to see him roll up to his father's farm in the dark. He was being sneaky, with his headlights off. I knew he must be meeting someone, so that was it. I deleted him from my phone, and I moved on. It's just a rather unfortunate coincidence that he happened to die the next day."

"You weren't angry about him seeing someone else?"

Tracy rolled her eyes. "Like I said, we weren't serious. I don't need drama in my life. If a guy wants to be with me, he can show it, otherwise there are plenty of others to choose from."

"Still, it must have bothered you that he lied."

"Is this where you say I killed him in a jealous rage?" Tracy laughed. "Sorry to disappoint you, ma'am, but I'm not the jealous type. Sure I followed him, but it was out of curiosity, not out of jealousy. I believe each person is entitled to their freedom."

"That's very modern of you."

She shrugged. "Life is hard enough without complicating it with love, right?"

"Right." Ally smiled a little at her words. "Still, I'm sorry for your loss."

"Thank you. I was pretty bummed to find out he was dead. Plus, my boss was irate that they shut down the farmer's market. That's a big day for us."

"You were there?"

"No, I wasn't. My boss was. Dan Savoy. He ran the booth at the farmer's market, while I kept the shop open here. Not that we had any customers."

"Thanks for your time, Tracy, I appreciate it."

As Ally walked out of the shop she made a mental note about Tracy not having an alibi. She could have easily left the shop if there were no customers. Maybe she seemed calm and casual when Ally spoke with her, but that didn't prove anything about her state of mind the day before.

Chapter Six

Ally drove to the chocolate shop. She pulled into the driveway and parked behind the store. With a quick tug she let herself in the back door.

"Mee-Maw, I'm here!"

"I'm out front, Ally."

Ally made her way through the storage area and past the kitchen where the chocolates and other chocolate delicacies were made. From the delicious scent of chocolate that hung in the air she knew that her grandmother had whipped up a fresh batch of chocolates. She stepped out into the front of the shop just in time to see her grandmother place a tray of chocolates on the shelf behind the counter.

"Oh, those look so good. How did you do all of that already?"

"We didn't have too many customers so I thought I'd put together a fresh selection. I want to get the sour taste of what happened at the farmer's market out of people's minds."

"Good idea. Do you want me to put them out on display?"

"Sure, that would be great. I think they are just cool enough. Here try one, they're toffee," Charlotte said as Ally popped one in her mouth.

"Yum!" Ally said while she chewed. "Not too sweet."

"Oh good, I thought so, too." Charlotte clapped her hands. "I'm going to clean up in the kitchen."

Ally walked over to the small sink beside the shelf and washed her hands. As she did she was reminded of the egg on Zac's shoes. After she dried her hands and put on gloves she began to place the chocolates on a display tray to put in the refrigerated cabinet. At almost the exact same moment the front door swung open. Mrs. Cale, Mrs. White, and Mrs. Bing filed inside. Ally smiled to herself as the women sniffed the air and hurried towards the counter.

"Oh Ally, these look delicious," Mrs. Cale said.

"Please, try some." Ally nudged the tray towards them. "They're toffee."

"My favorite!" Mrs. Bing squeaked and snatched up one of the chocolates. The other two women followed suit. "Mmm, very good." Mrs. Bing nodded and sucked on the chocolate.

"Have you heard the latest about Nigel? It looks like his brother is the one who killed him." Mrs. White shook her head. "Isn't it awful?"

"It's hard to conceive of a brother killing a brother." Ally frowned.

"Especially Colin and Nigel." Mrs. Cale held up a finger in the air. "When they were boys I never once saw Colin without his brother. He took that little boy everywhere, especially after their mother died. I guess Bob was just too busy on the farm. But Nigel and Colin were together most of the time. I can't believe that Colin would ever kill him."

Ally saw her opportunity to learn more about

Nigel's life and took it. "What I don't understand is why Nigel was working at Tyler's farm, instead of his father's." Ally decided to try and get more information.

"You don't know why?" Mrs. Bing raised an eyebrow. "I think that you missed a lot while you were away."

"I guess I did." Ally rested her chin on her hand. "Care to fill me in?"

"Yes, absolutely." Mrs. White cleared her throat. "So, Bob and Tyler were very close in high school. Everyone knew if they messed with one then they had to deal with the other. They both had plans to run their father's farms, right next door to one another, and even talked about raising their families together. I mean everyone in town knew they were inseparable. They might as well have been brothers."

"So, what happened?" Ally frowned.

"Well, Bob fell on some hard times. He was really struggling financially after his wife died. Tyler offered to buy some of Bob's land so that the taxes wouldn't be so high for him. Bob agreed. There was a verbal agreement that the land would be returned to Bob once Bob had the money to pay Tyler back," Mrs. White said. "However, Tyler decided to take actual ownership of the land and keep it, supposedly despite the fact that Bob had the money and wanted to pay him back every penny. Tyler refused to sell the land back to Bob. There was one fight in the middle of town and then Bob never spoke to Tyler again."

"Wow." Ally straightened up. "He took advantage of a widow?"

"With two young sons. He always was a cunning businessman, but I think that move shocked the whole town." Mrs. White shook her head.

"That still doesn't explain why Nigel was at Tyler's farm," Ally said.

"All of that started when Bob got remarried. I guess Nigel expected him to stay single for the rest of his life. Nigel had a big problem with the new wife. He even claimed that she cheated on Bob.

But of course, he never had any proof. I just assumed he was trying to break them up, a very jealous son competing for his father's attention," Mrs. White said.

"Oh please, Bob never gave that boy any attention. As to liking the new wife, who would? She's new money, classless, and a gold digger to boot." Mrs. Cale huffed.

"Now, now, that's not nice." Mrs. White shook her head. "There are much wealthier places to dig for gold than in Bob's pockets. It's not like he's rich. He has lots of property and likes to act rich, but he is up to his ears in debt."

"He has done well over the past few years." Mrs. Bing snapped her fingers. "Except this last crop I've heard was nearly lost."

"Wait a minute, ladies, can we go back to why Nigel was working at Tyler's farm?" Ally asked.

"Oh right, yes." Mrs. Bing nodded. "Nigel and his father had a falling out over the new wife. Either Nigel quit the farm or Bob fired him, no one's really sure. Then Nigel disappeared for a week or two. When he turned up he took a job at Tyler's farm. It was quite the scandal. What kind of son betrays his father like that?"

"Nigel didn't owe that man anything." Mrs. White shook her head. "If Bob had been a father to that boy, then he never would have acted that way."

"Parenting is not as easy as it seems." Mrs. Cale sighed. "I guess it doesn't really matter now."

"You're right." Mrs. Bing pursed her lips. "We're eating candy and gossiping, and a young man is dead."

All three women fell silent. Then Mrs. Cale snatched a chocolate from the tray. Her two friends turned reproachful looks on her.

"What? I stopped gossiping didn't I?" She popped the chocolate into her mouth. Soon her friends followed suit.

Charlotte wiped her hands clean as she stepped out from the back room. She smiled at the three women.

"Did you like those?" Charlotte asked.

"Oh yes." Mrs. White smiled.

"Thank you so much." Mrs. Cale nodded.

"Do you have any more?" Mrs. Bing peered through the open door that led to the back.

"I promise to have more soon." Charlotte smiled. "I'm glad you like the new recipe."

"It's perfect." Mrs. White dropped a few dollars on the counter.

"No charge." Charlotte picked up the money and handed it back to Mrs. White.

"Oh, thank you." Mrs. White tucked the money back into her purse. As the three women left Ally turned to look at her grandmother.

"They ate the whole tray, again." Ally frowned.

"Yes, they did. But they also gave you lots of information. I was just trying them out. It means more to me to have three loyal customers than it does to have a few dollars in the register."

"I know." Ally smiled. "It just seems like a lot of chocolates to give away."

"But it's worth it. It's time to close up." Charlotte walked over to the front door and turned the open sign to closed, then turned to look at Ally. "I overheard most of your conversation, what do you think?"

"I'm not sure, Mee-Maw. Everyone seems to think that Colin clearly committed the murder, but I think that he was least likely to do it. He loved his brother, he practically raised him. Bob and Tyler had plenty of anger and resentment between them. But Nigel and Colin didn't have that same friction. How could one argument lead to murder?"

"I think that it's always hard to understand murder. The thing is that Colin and his brother were at war. If what the ladies say is true, Nigel worked on the farm of a man who essentially robbed Bob."

"But were they really at war?" Ally wiped down the counter while Charlotte shut down the cash register. "Even though the press has portrayed them as enemies, the way Colin spoke about his brother told me that he understood his brother and forgave him. It sounds to me that the problem was more between Nigel and his father. I would expect, as Colin claimed to be doing, that he would try to mend the rift between his father and brother. However, his father was missing in action during the time of the murder and he had plenty of motive. Maybe he just couldn't take the betrayal anymore."

"But you heard what Colin's father said as we left the house. He was very angry. Maybe he found out about what Colin did. He might have been angry at his son for leaving the farm, but surely he would have been furious with Colin if he killed Nigel."

"True." Ally shook her head. "But again, why would Colin kill him? It's not like they even suffered on the farm. Nigel was replaced by Zac, who knew just as much about working the farm as Nigel. What motive did Colin have?"

"I suppose if Colin tried to reconcile and Nigel refused that could be motive."

"I guess." Ally grabbed a broom and swept the floor in the front area of the shop. "I just think that two brothers who were that close would need more than a family argument to drive them apart and result in murder."

"You may be right. In fact, now that you mention Zac, he may be a suspect, too. Remember you saw egg on his shoe."

"Yes, but his shoes were clean when I saw him today. I asked him today if there were any chickens on Bob's farm, he said yes. Also, I don't know what his motive would be."

"Maybe he was afraid that if Nigel came back into the fold he would lose his new position at the farm. Colin mentioned that Zac got a pay rise when he took over Nigel's place. That might not have been something that he wanted to lose."

"That would be a terrible reason to kill someone." Ally set the broom against the wall and looked over at her grandmother. "Supposedly, they were friends for a long time."

"Yes, it would, but people have been killed for much less." Charlotte locked the cash register and joined Ally in front of the counter. "Zac might have enjoyed taking on the role of prince at Bob's farm. What about the girlfriend? You said she could have done it, too?"

"She had the opportunity, but I don't know what motive. Unless she is very good at hiding it, she didn't seem to have any feelings at all for Nigel. I just hope there's a way to get to the bottom of all of this. And hopefully before Colin is arrested."

As they walked out to the car, Ally glanced back in the direction of the shop. She wondered if she would be able to maintain its reputation in the community the way Charlotte had. One thing was for sure, she had a lot to learn from her grandmother.

Chapter Seven

Ally drove Charlotte to Freely Lakes. It still felt strange that her grandmother did not live at the cottage with her. But that night she was relieved to have some alone time, as her mind ached with the labyrinth of the case. Nigel, a young man who barely had the opportunity to make his mark on the world, was dead, and there were a few people who could have killed him.

After Ally had dropped off her grandmother and said goodnight she drove back to the cottage. As soon as she opened the door she was greeted by two hungry animals. Arnold had kicked his water dish over and splashed in it all across the kitchen floor. Peaches was curled up on the kitchen counter, as she did not like to get her paws wet. Ally mopped up the floor and fed them both. Then she leaned against the kitchen counter and stared out the window at the fading evening light.

As Ally sorted through each person she had spoken to, she knew there was a problem. There were two people that she hadn't exchanged a word with. Bob, and his wife, Linda. Considering their family history if they had no alibi for the time of the murder they were prime suspects. She pulled out her phone to call Luke and see if he had heard anything else, but before she could dial the number her phone began to ring. She smiled when she saw it was Luke.

"I was just thinking of you," Ally said.

"Oh? Don't take this the wrong way, but so was I."

"Why would I take that the wrong way?"

"Because the reason I called is not exactly personal," Luke said.

"What is it?"

"I was able to get some information out of one of the Mainbry detectives that is working on the case. The medical examiner found that not only was Nigel killed by a wound to his chest, most probably caused by a hay knife, he was not killed where he was found."

"Wow." Ally's eyes widened. "That means that someone moved him?"

"Yes, it does. It makes more sense doesn't it? How could someone have not witnessed the murder if it happened behind the booth?"

"Sure, it does make more sense. But how could someone move a body around a busy farmer's market without being caught?"

"That part I'm not sure about. But at least it's a step in the right direction."

"I hope so." Ally sighed and looked back out the window. "I feel like there's not much to go on. I really need to speak with Bob and Linda."

"That's going to be tough."

"That's where you come in."

"Why do I think I'm not going to like this?"

"Don't you want to spend some quality time with me, Luke?"

"Ally, what do you have up your sleeve?"

"Well, I know that Bob and Linda won't speak

106

to some random woman who runs a chocolate store. He strikes me as a very private person. Luckily for me, I know someone with a badge."

"Ally, I'm not working this case. I'm not allowed to. Remember?"

"I know, and I know it would be asking a lot. But all you would have to do is introduce me as a consultant, flash your badge, and I'm sure they will comply with questioning. You wouldn't even have to give them your name or what police department you're with. I can't think of another way to get in to see them. I suppose I could break in and..."

"No." His voice was so stern that Ally raised an eyebrow.

"Excuse me?"

"Ally, you can't break into the Dean house. If you get caught you're looking at definite jail time. These people are wealthy, even if they had some financial struggles, their reputation and history in Mainbry makes them elite. If you are caught invading their home the Mainbry police will have you behind bars in no time, and there won't be anything that I can do to help you."

"I see what you're saying." She sighed. "What about flashing your badge."

"My badge is not a toy," Luke said. "I will not risk it."

"All right, I understand," Ally said. "I guess both plans have their flaws. What do you think I should do?"

"I think that you should stay out of this."

"I can't."

"You have to," Luke said. "I'll see what I can find out, but you need to take a step back."

"But Luke, I can't let an innocent man go to jail for a crime he didn't commit."

"Ally, the truth will come out, but you cannot put yourself at risk and I am not going to put my badge at risk."

"Of course, I don't want you to do that."

"You need to stay out of this."

"Okay," Ally said but she had no intention of staying out of it. She needed to find out the truth and now that she thought about it properly, she knew that she couldn't get Luke involved. She couldn't put Luke's job at risk.

"I hope you understand."

"Of course, Luke." She did understand, she just needed to come up with a plan so Luke wasn't involved.

"Hopefully you'll still dance with me."

Ally laughed. "Good night."

"Good night. Sleep well."

When he hung up the phone Ally's mind started racing. She needed a plan to get to talk to Bob and Linda. The only thing she could come up with were chocolates and her grandmother's charm. She just needed a way to convince her grandmother to come with her.

Ally tossed a few things together for dinner and settled on the couch. Within moments Peaches was perched on the back of the couch with one paw on Ally's shoulder. Though Ally didn't have a lot of family, she certainly felt surrounded by love. She wondered if Nigel ever had the luxury of feeling that way.

Ally closed her eyes and pictured Colin as the killer. He could have easily killed Nigel with the hay knife. Then he could have moved his brother's body behind the stand. How was it that no one saw any of it?

Her eyes opened as she recalled the man who ran the booth beside Nigel's. He claimed he saw Nigel go back to the barn for eggs, but never saw him come back. Ally assumed he was lying for some reason or was mistaken, but what if he just didn't know that he saw Nigel come back? If Nigel's body was somehow hidden, the man in the next booth might have seen the whole thing, but the police didn't ask the right questions. Ally grabbed her phone and called her grandmother. She picked up with the sound of laughter in the background.

"Mee-Maw? Is someone with you?"

"Oh, I'm just playing cards." Her voice was warm. Ally narrowed her eyes.

"Sorry to interrupt, I just have a couple of questions."

"Sure, what is it?"

"Do you know the man who ran the booth next to Nigel's? The man who told you Nigel went for eggs?"

"Yes, it's Harry. Harry Tuck. He's been working at Mainbry Apple Orchard for years. That's about twenty minutes from here."

Ally glanced at the clock. "It's probably closed for the night."

"I would imagine so."

"Do you know him well?"

"No, only from buying apples from the orchard. He's a very private person. Do you think he had something to do with all of this?"

"No, but I think he might have seen more than he knows. Thanks, Mee-Maw."

"Call me if you need me, Ally. I'm always here for you."

"I know you are. That leads me to my next question. Will you come with me to deliver some chocolates to Bob and Linda tomorrow?"

"Okay, but I get the feeling that this isn't a social visit."

"I'll pick you up at eight and I'll fill you in on the way."

"I'll be ready."

"What is Linda's favorite chocolate?"

"Milk hazelnut."

"Great, we have some at the shop. I'll pick up a box of them on the way to you tomorrow."

"Good idea, but mix in some others in case Bob doesn't like them. Linda always buys a variety."

"Okay, I'll let you get back to your card game. Have fun!"

"Thanks, sweetie. See you in the morning."

Ally hung up and called Luke back. She waited through several rings before he answered.

"Sorry, Ally I'm in the middle of something."

"Okay, but real quick, do you know anything about Harry Tuck, the man who ran the booth beside Nigel's? It was Mainbry Apple Orchard's booth."

"No, sorry. I have to go we're about to make a bust."

"Okay, okay sorry." Ally hung up the phone. She couldn't help but smile a little that Luke answered the phone at such an important moment, but she felt a little guilty that she had interrupted. She looked up Harry Tuck on the Mainbry community page. As she hoped his name and address were listed. Since she would be going with her grandmother first thing in the morning, she thought it would be a good idea to meet with Harry that night. It wasn't too late yet, and she hoped that he would be willing to talk.

"Peaches, I'm going to find out the truth no matter how hard I have to look." She stroked the cat's head and back. "Colin lost his brother, and he deserves to know why." She gave the cat a quick peck on the cheek then grabbed her keys.

As Ally drove towards the address she found on the community page she rehearsed what she might say to Harry. When she parked outside of a small trailer her heart dropped. The front yard was littered with trash and scrapped appliances. Although the trailer on the property was nice, it seemed to her that Harry had no interest in the upkeep of the property. She had seen this type of yard before and knew better than to assume he was lazy. The people she'd encountered with this type of mess, kept it that way because they wanted their privacy and did not like visitors. That meant that Harry was not likely to want to talk. She picked her way carefully up to the door of the trailer as the sun was almost down. When she knocked on the trailer door she heard the television inside turn off.

"Who is it?" His hard voice made her even less hopeful.

"Mr. Tuck?"

"Mister?" He laughed as he opened the door. "It's too late at night for bill collectors and pamphlets, who are you, little lady?"

Ally was relieved that he was at least friendly, but when she took a step closer she found out why. She could smell the alcohol on him.

"My name is Ally. I was hoping you could answer a few questions for me."

"Questions about what?" He gestured for her to come inside the trailer. Ally planted one hand on the door of the trailer to make sure that she would stay right where she was.

"I'm sorry, I'm in a bit of a rush. It's really only one question."

"Then shoot, girlie, I'm missing my program." He coughed and put his hand on the door right above hers.

"It's about Nigel Dean."

"Oh, him again? People don't let a dead man rest in this town do they?" He shook his head.

"Nigel's dead. Nothing more to it. I knew that kid was going to cause me trouble."

"Well, someone killed him, there's that."

"I don't know anything about that. I tried to get my booth moved away from his in fact."

"Why is that?"

"I don't like drama. I'm a simple man. I want to go to work, come home and watch my programs. That's all. When I was at the farm signing up for my booth a little over a week ago now, I overheard this young couple arguing. I think the guy was one of Bob's farmhands. He was with that cute dame that works in the flower shop. Anyway, they were arguing about Nigel. I guess she was dating him. But the guy told her Nigel slept with his stepmother. Then the girl got all upset. I knew that was a mess just waiting to happen. Not that it's any of my business, but my money's on the girl."

"Did you happen to see her at the farmer's market that day?"

"No, I didn't. But I saw Bob's guy there again. He walked right past Nigel's booth. Nigel called out to him, Zac I think he called him, but Zac just kept walking."

"You mentioned seeing Nigel go to the barn. But his body was found behind the counter of his booth. You don't think that's odd?"

"Look, like I told the detective. I'm a drinker. I was drinking that day, too. I could have sworn Nigel went to the barn, and I never saw him come back, but obviously I was wrong and he did come back. Is it a crime to be drunk now?"

Ally raised an eyebrow. "I tend to believe you weren't that drunk."

"What makes you think that?"

"You were at work."

"So?"

"So, I bet you don't drink as much at work as you do at home."

"Well, that's true." He shrugged. "So what?"

"So, can you see me standing here?"

"Is this some kind of game?" He narrowed his eyes. "I told you, I'm missing my program."

"It's not a game. I'm just making a point. The police want to claim you were too drunk to know what you saw. But I venture to guess that you are more drunk now than you were then, and you see me just fine don't you?"

"Sure I do." He smiled in a lustful way that revealed he was missing a few teeth. Ally gritted her teeth against the quick fear that rushed through her. Solving a murder meant taking a few risks, but she might have miscalculated on this one. She slid her hand into her pocket and held onto her phone so at least it was close if she needed to call for help.

"Maybe you just didn't know that you saw Nigel come back. What about someone carrying a large bag?"

"A large bag?" He shook his head. "No. But wait, I did see something a little odd. This guy was pushing a large wheelbarrow with a big ratty blanket in it. I thought it was strange because he pushed it straight up to the booths instead of taking it along the tractor path. I figured it was one of Tyler's guys. I had a few customers and when I looked back he was gone. You think Nigel was in the wheelbarrow?"

"I think it's possible." Ally smiled. "What about the man? Can you describe him?"

"Not really. He wore a big hat, didn't see his face. I did find it strange that he was wearing a jacket in the warm weather. Of course he wasn't so lovely to look at, not like you." He smiled at her again.

"Thanks for your time, Mr. Tuck."

"Mister." He laughed again and then slammed his door shut. As Ally hurried back to her car she wondered just who had pushed that wheelbarrow. And if Zac knew that Nigel had a girlfriend, Tracy, why hadn't he told Ally when she had asked? Also, was Zac telling the truth about Nigel having an affair with his stepmother? If so that placed Bob and Linda right back at the top of the suspect list. She was eager to speak to them tomorrow morning.

When Ally got back to the cottage she had a quick shower and climbed into bed. Peaches hopped into bed with her. Ally pet the cat as she stared into the dark. In her mind she went through what she knew about the murder. It was clear now that Nigel's body had been moved. She even knew how it was moved. But that still didn't tell her who killed him or where he was killed.

There were many open fields around the farmer's market, but that would have been a very visible place to commit the crime, but it was still possible. If Nigel went back to the barn to get more eggs as Harry claimed, then that was a perfect place for the murder to happen. Maybe someone met up with Nigel in the barn. They used a hay knife to commit the murder. Then they piled him up in a wheelbarrow, covered him with a blanket, and tossed him behind the booth. That was probably how the eggs were broken. If Nigel had any left at the stand his body probably fell on them.

There would not have been a commotion and on the busy farm no one would have thought twice about a man pushing a wheelbarrow. She turned over in her bed and pulled Peaches close. If that was the case then the crime of passion might not have been a crime of passion. It might have been a premeditated, cold-blooded murder. But what was the motive? Who was the murderer?

Chapter Eight

When Ally woke the next morning she only had a few minutes to get dressed before she had to pick up her grandmother. The shop didn't open until ten so they would have plenty of time to speak to Bob and Linda before she needed to be there to open it. She rushed around to feed the cat, the pig, and herself. However, when she went to get the pig feed out she noticed how light it was. In all of the commotion she had forgotten to buy more. She filled Arnold's bowl with what was left of the emergency supply.

"Sorry buddy. I promise I will pick some up for you today." She tossed the bag in the trash and picked up her keys. She hurried to her car and drove to the chocolate shop to pick up a box of chocolates for Linda and Bob.

Then she drove as quickly as she could without breaking the speed limit to Freely Lakes to pick up her grandmother. As she drove there she thought about what she would ask Bob and

Linda.

When Ally pulled up her grandmother was just walking out the front door. She smiled at Ally as she opened the passenger side door.

"Wow, right on time. Not a second late," Charlotte said.

"Morning Mee-Maw," Ally said.

"Did you find out anything else about the murder?"

"Well, I had an interesting visit with Harry last night."

"Harry?" Charlotte looked over at her. "Wait a minute, you mean Harry Tuck?"

"Yes." Ally nodded.

"You went to see him last night?" Charlotte stared at her across the car. "By yourself?"

"I had some questions for him. He gave me a lot of information actually, including that Nigel had an affair with Linda." She glanced over at her with a satisfied smile. "That's a surprise, right?"

"It is! But you shouldn't have gone there alone."

"He was pretty harmless." Ally shrugged. She decided to keep the details to herself as she didn't want to upset her grandmother.

"I still don't think you should do things like that," Charlotte said. "It makes me worried. You should have got me to come with you."

"You were busy and I can take care of myself." Ally smiled. "I promise."

"I'm not trying to tell you what to do, Ally. I know that would never work, it never has. But I am always available for you, dear."

She couldn't help but smile at her grandmother's words. "I know that, Mee-Maw, but I didn't think it was that big of a deal, so I just went and checked things out."

"But you didn't have to do it. You can be a little impulsive, Ally," Charlotte said. "I just worry that it can put you in danger."

"You're right. I tend to be a bit impulsive. But

I'm glad that I did go. Because he was drunk and talkative."

"Oh, that makes me feel a lot better."

"The important thing is that I'm fine." Ally smiled at her. Charlotte shook her head, but offered her a smile in return. For the remainder of the drive Ally filled her in on what she planned to talk to the Deans about. "We need to try and get Linda alone so we can work out if Nigel and her were really having an affair."

"Just tread carefully, sweetheart," Charlotte said.

"I will, of course. I'm also going to ask about the coffee shop. Okay?"

"Yes. I think that's a good idea." Ally picked up the chocolate box, stepped out of the car and walked towards her grandmother. When she reached her grandmother Colin walked towards the car.

"He hasn't been arrested yet," Ally said in a hushed voice to her grandmother.

Ally smiled at Colin as he walked up to her. "Ally, I wasn't expecting to see you today." He glanced over at Charlotte. "Morning Charlotte."

"We just wanted to have a quick word to your father and stepmother. Give them some chocolates," Ally said.

"I think that you should reconsider. My dad is not in the best of moods. He just found out that it's likely someone is intentionally poisoning our crops."

"I'm sorry to hear that. Do you think Nigel might have been involved?" Ally recalled what Tracy said about Nigel sneaking on to his father's farm.

"No way." Colin shook his head. "Nigel might have been angry at my father, but he would never do anything to hurt the farm. It may look like a piece of land to you, but to us, it's a part of our beings. It's got our blood, sweat, tears, all mixed into the soil, not to mention the only memories Nigel and I have of our mother. I know my brother would never have done anything to harm this land."

"Then maybe he knew who was?" Ally glanced across the field.

"Maybe. As I mentioned he did say he wanted to talk to me and my father about something important the day he died. But like I said, today would not be a good day to talk to my father about it."

Ally frowned. "Colin, we just want to drop off the chocolates and see if he knows anything that will help solve the murder."

"Just be gentle, he's in a shocking mood," Colin said. Ally wondered if Bob was often in a shocking mood and made enemies.

"If your father is hiding something it's going to have to come out. You want your brother to have justice don't you?"

Colin sighed and retreated a step. "Yes. I do. But I can't be involved in this."

"You don't have to be." Ally smiled at him. "As far as you're concerned you never saw us today."

She tilted her head towards the path that led to the fields. "We'll be gone before you get back."

Colin frowned and met her eyes. "Ally, this is my family."

"I know it is, Colin. I will remember that. I promise."

He nodded and then walked down the path. Ally started to walk towards the main house, but Charlotte grabbed her gently by the wrist.

"Just be subtle," Charlotte said.

"I will be, I promise."

Ally and Charlotte continued towards the house.

When Ally knocked on the front door it took some time for anyone to answer. When someone did, it was Linda. She looked impeccable in a light blue dress with high-heeled sandals to match. As soon as she saw Ally and Charlotte she smiled, she looked a little confused.

"Morning Linda," Charlotte said. "This is my granddaughter, Ally."

"Nice to meet you," Linda's smile grew wider.

"Linda, we just wanted to give you these," Charlotte said as she handed her the chocolates. They include your favorite, the milk hazelnut chocolates, as well as a few others."

"Oh, thank you. That's so sweet," Linda said. "How much do I owe you?"

"Nothing," Charlotte said and shook her head. "I just wanted to give you something during this trying time."

"Thank you."

"We were wondering if we could see Mr. Dean as well, to express our condolences," Charlotte said.

"Okay sure," Linda said hesitantly. "I'll see if he's available."

Linda ushered Charlotte inside. She was followed by Ally. Linda showed them to a small study.

"I'll just go see if he's free," Linda said as she walked out of the room. Once the door closed, Ally turned to Charlotte.

"The secret power of chocolate." Ally smiled.

"Clever thinking, Ally," Charlotte said.

As they waited Ally decided to snoop around the study. There were several pictures on the shelves of the brothers when they were young as well as with their mother. She smiled fondly at the sight of one where Colin was wrapped in her arms. A pang of grief struck her. Not only did Colin lose his mother at a young age, as she had, but he also lost his brother. It was no surprise to her that he was protective of his father. They turned towards the door as it swung open. Bob stepped inside with Linda on his arm.

"What is this about?" Ally turned to face him. Bob narrowed his eyes. "I remember you. You were here talking to my son."

"Yes, I was," Ally said.

"We are sorry for your loss," Charlotte said. Bob didn't respond he just looked angry.

"Thank you again. These chocolates look

delicious," Linda said softly trying to break the tension. "I'll get us some drinks." She started to leave the study.

"If you don't mind, Linda, I just had a question for both of you," Ally said.

Bob crossed his arms. "What question?" Linda wrapped her arm around her husband's.

"Where were you and Linda at the time of your son's death?"

"At the coffee shop," Bob said. "Why is it important I already told the police this?"

"We were having a coffee." Linda smiled. "We were sharing a pastry as well."

"Was it Mainbry Café?" Ally looked between the two of them.

"Yes, that's where we always go. What does it matter?" Bob said.

"It matters, Sir, because Mainbry Café was closed on the day of the farmer's market. It's not possible that you were there."

Bob's face tensed. "Well, then we must have

gone to a different one."

"Which one do you think?" Ally narrowed her eyes. "Maybe you have a receipt from the shop?"

"Never mind that nonsense. What are you implying? That I may have had something to do with my son's murder?" His voice raised with every word that he spoke. Charlotte moved closer to Ally.

"I'm not implying that at all, Sir. I just wondered why you would say you were there if you weren't," Ally said.

"I don't have to answer this," Bob replied.

"Why would you lie?" Ally asked.

Linda sighed. "Just tell them, Bob. It's no big deal."

"Invasion of privacy is always a big deal." Bob shook his head.

"You even lied to your oldest son, Colin." Ally lifted an eyebrow. "Why?"

"Because no son likes to hear that his parents are holed up in the car having some fun, okay?"

Bob rolled his eyes. "Linda and I hadn't had much alone time together in a while and after our tour of the farm we were a little frisky..."

"Farm equipment does it to Bob every time." Linda winked. "Something about the roar of the tractor I think."

"Linda. That's more than they need to know," Bob said impatiently.

"Sorry." She grimaced. "The point is, we were having some private time, and Colin didn't need to know about that."

Ally felt awful and slightly embarrassed.

"Now, please leave," Bob said. "I've had a terrible morning and I didn't kill my son."

Ally was about to object but Charlotte jumped in. "Of course. We didn't mean to intrude."

Charlotte grabbed Ally's arm and guided her towards the front of the house. Linda followed after them.

"Thanks again for the chocolates, Charlotte," Linda said.

"I'm sorry we imposed on you." Charlotte frowned.

"Linda, I don't mean to talk about private things, but there is a rumor going around that there was something going on between you and Nigel," Ally said softly, trying to sound casual and not accusing.

The color drained from Linda's face. "We didn't get along that's all. He missed his mother."

"Really? Because I heard there was more to your relationship than that," Ally said. "I heard that you were having an affair."

"That is complete nonsense!"

"Are you sure because it is certainly going around," Ally said.

"It's complicated. It's not what you think," Linda whispered.

"So you did have an affair," Ally asked.

"It was over so quickly," Linda said as she steered them further away from the study. "I love Bob."

"Does Bob know?" Ally asked quietly.

"Of course not. He would never understand." She got tears in her eyes. "It wasn't my fault. It was before I even met Bob. I didn't know Nigel was his son until we were engaged."

"You've managed to keep it from him all of this time?" Ally asked with surprise.

"I've had to. You can't tell him." She begged in a soft voice.

"Don't worry we won't," Charlotte said.

"He chose me over his son. He would never forgive me." Tears rolled down Linda's cheeks. Bob walked out into the hallway.

"What are they still doing here?" he demanded pointing at Charlotte and Ally.

"We were just leaving," Charlotte said.

"What's wrong?" Bob put his arm around Linda who was crying. "Did they upset you?"

"No, I'm just upset about Nigel." Her voice wavered over every word.

"Why did you upset her? Leave now!" Bob demanded.

"Don't worry we're going." Charlotte grabbed Ally's hand and led her out of the house.

"I hope Linda's okay," Ally said as they walked quickly towards the car.

"Hey, wait a minute!" A man waved to them from the nearby barn. Ally froze near the door and then turned to look back at the man. She squinted to see if she recognized him. She couldn't recall seeing him before. Charlotte turned towards him. The man jogged up to them then paused a few feet away.

"Bruce, what can we do for you?" Charlotte asked.

"I heard that you've been asking a lot of questions about Nigel's death," he said quickly.

"Do you have some information?" Ally shifted from one foot to the other and lifted her chin.

"Yes, I think I do."

"What is it?" Charlotte asked.

"It's about Zac. I noticed something about him. Look, the detectives that were here, they seemed bent on their idea of what happened. I just don't want to get involved in the investigation. But this has been bugging me ever since Nigel turned up dead." He frowned. "I don't really know if I should say something or not, but I feel like if I don't, I'll regret it."

"What is it?" Charlotte leaned closer to him.

"You can tell us," Ally said, she was so intrigued. "It won't be linked to you."

"Are you sure?" He looked from Ally back to Charlotte. "I mean, if Zac finds out it was me that outed him, I don't think he's going to like it very much."

"It's going to be just fine, Bruce. Just tell us what happened," Charlotte said sweetly.

"The thing is Zac got promoted, and sure that comes with a salary bump, but the money he has been flashing around is more than he could be making on his salary."

"What do you mean by flashing?" Ally asked.

"I mean wads of cash, everywhere he goes he whips out a wallet stacked with hundreds. When he gets drunk he starts buying rounds for everyone in the bar. He acts like he's a millionaire." He shook his head. "There's just no way that could be right."

"Where do you think he's getting the money from?" Charlotte raised an eyebrow.

"All I know is that he's been going over to Tyler's farm on a regular basis."

"We know that he was meeting with Nigel." Ally looked up at him. "Isn't that why he's been going to Tyler's farm?"

"No, I know he wasn't going there to meet Nigel every time. It was always late at night, or early in the morning when Nigel either would have been in bed or out in the fields. Plus a few times that I've seen Zac sneak off over there, I've seen Nigel at the same time, alone. I don't think he was going there to meet Nigel."

"Then why?" Ally looked in his eyes. "Who else would he be meeting with?"

"I think someone's been paying him off."

"Paying him off for what? Does he know something he shouldn't?" Ally thought back through what she knew about the murder to try to figure out who Zac might be blackmailing.

"I think he's getting paid to do things that he shouldn't be doing. What those things are, I can't be sure. But I know if he was getting that kind of money it had to be something illegal."

"And you think he was involved with the murder somehow?" Ally looked back up at him.

"I don't know. I mean Zac had a temper sometimes. Sure Nigel and Zac were best friends, but they were different, you know?"

"Different how?" Charlotte prompted.

"Nigel could get frustrated, but he always had this moral code that he followed. When we would all go out for drinks he was the type of guy to stay sober to keep an eye on all of us. Drive us home.

When a few of the guys would get into fights he would always find a peaceful way to settle the disputes. Zac is the type of guy that will do anything to get ahead. He came from just about nothing, and he's thirsty to be rich. He wants that life. I don't know why. I like the simple things myself. But Zac was always trying to come up with some way to get rich. I just have a feeling that maybe Zac was up to something illegal, maybe Nigel found out about it. Of course I don't know that for sure. It's just something that's been bugging me. I'm not even sure if any of this will help. But you know, Nigel was a good guy. He helped me out more than once, and I hate to see his murder go unsolved."

"And what about Colin?" Ally took a step closer to him. "Did you ever see Colin and Nigel fight?"

"Not until everything went sour, when that woman moved in. Before that Colin and Nigel were always at each other's sides. I rarely saw one without the other. That's the thing. Colin would never do this to Nigel, there's no way. Maybe it wasn't Zac either, but I know for a fact it wasn't Colin."

"Thanks, you've been a big help to us," Ally said.

"Please just keep my name out of this. All right? In fact, you're better off forgetting we ever had this conversation. If you're able to get somewhere because of it, that's great, but the information never came from me. Don't want to lose my job and certainly don't want to lose my life. Understand?"

"Yes." Ally nodded.

As he walked away Ally turned to Charlotte.

"You know him?"

"Yes but not very well, he moved to Mainbry with his parents about five years ago. I don't know if we can completely trust the information he's given to us. I don't know if he's changed, but I know he was arrested a couple of years ago for stealing. His parents' work at the hardware store in town. They are private but nice enough."

"Do you think he had something to do with Nigel's death?" Ally asked.

"Maybe, I don't like judging people by their history, but I think he was way too eager to give us the information."

"We can look into him more, but presuming the information he gave us was correct I think we need to talk to Tyler and find out if Zac was actually meeting with someone at the farm and if he was, whether he knows who he was meeting with."

"I think you're right, but not now," Charlotte said. "We need to open the shop."

"Can't we just swing by Tyler's farm first?" Ally asked. "It's just the next farm over."

"No, we'll be late and it's a short opening day today anyway."

"You're right," Ally said as she started the car and drove off Bob's property. "We certainly found out a lot of information."

"That, we did." Charlotte smiled.

"So, what do you think about Linda and Bob?" Ally asked.

"I don't think he knows about the affair which means that wasn't his motive."

"No, me neither," Ally agreed. "Like she said he chose her over his son."

"Unless, he found out about it recently and he was so angry he killed Nigel."

"It's a definite possibility."

"But now we know that the affair is a reality not just a rumor, Linda certainly has a motive."

"Yes, that's exactly what I was thinking." Ally nodded as they pulled up to the shop.

"Right on time," Charlotte said as she looked at her watch.

Ally opened the shop but all her mind could do was sort through the details of the murder.

Chapter Nine

After they had locked up for the day and Ally had dropped Charlotte off at Freely Lakes she headed home. She pulled up outside the cottage just as her phone rang. She saw it was Luke and answered quickly.

"Hi, Luke."

"Hi, I'm still working, but I just wanted to check in and see how you're going."

"Good, I found out a few interesting things today."

"Oh, I hope you haven't been getting into too much trouble."

"No, but I want to speak to Tyler, apparently Zac's been having meetings with someone at Tyler's farm. I want to see what Tyler knows about it."

"How do you know that?"

"When I went to see Bob and Linda this

morning..."

"What? You went even though I told you not to."

"I just wanted to pay my respects." Ally spoke quickly so Luke couldn't interrupt again. "Someone working on Bob's farm just came over and told us that Zac was meeting with someone on Tyler's farm."

"Really?" Luke asked skeptically.

"Absolutely."

"I think you need to be very careful. Let the Mainbry police handle this. I don't think you should talk to Tyler."

"Okay." Ally tried to change the subject. "How did the bust go last night?"

"It was a bust."

"I know, but how did it go?"

"I mean, the bust was a bust." He laughed. "Nothing there but a bunch of dirty rabbit cages."

"Ew. I bet that wasn't a fun thing to find."

"No, it certainly wasn't. I definitely needed a shower." He shook his head. "For anyone that thinks law enforcement is about glory, they need to be faced with what I saw last night."

"I'm glad I didn't see it."

"You would have been," Luke said. "I have to go. I have to work late. Stay safe, please."

"I will."

Ally got out of the car and opened the cottage door. When she was inside the cottage she tried to focus on the facts of the case and sort through everything. When that didn't work and she couldn't think clearly, she tried to coax Peaches into playing. She waved her favorite string around. She tossed her bell ball. Peaches stared at the ball as it skidded across the floor. Then she looked up at Ally and blinked.

"I know, I know. I'm not in the mood for this either." Ally sighed and picked her up. She carried her to the couch. The moment that she sat down Peaches settled on her lap. Ally stroked Peaches' soft fur and chewed her bottom lip.

"I know that I should stay right here, Peaches, but doesn't every second count? Isn't there always a good reason to investigate?" She smoothed back the fur on the top of the cat's head. Peaches looked up at her and sniffed. "Yes, I know. Mee-Maw said she will go with me later. But that's later. That's not right now." She scratched the underside of Peaches' chin. "Would it really be that big of a deal if I just went over there to speak to Tyler real quick?" Peaches meowed rather loudly.

"Oh, you too?" Ally frowned. "I can take care of myself you know. Besides, Arnold has to eat. I need to get over there while the stand is still open or I might not get any food." She smiled and scooted Peaches off her lap. "See, I have no choice, I have to go." She left out the fact that that was not the only place she could buy pig food. Peaches wound her way around Ally's feet as if she might try to stop her. But Ally was used to her cat's antics and easily sidestepped her. As she grabbed her purse she thought about texting Luke or her grandmother to let them know where she was going. But she didn't want to deal with an argument. She was just going to buy pig feed, that was all. She would be careful. She repeated these things in her mind as she walked to her car, got in, and began to drive.

Her heart fluttered a little once she was on the road. She hoped that she would be able to find out something from Tyler before it was too late and Colin was arrested. She rounded the corner to the front of the farm and pulled up to the dusty roadside stand. She again considered whether she should text Luke to let him know what she was doing. But she decided not to, she only had the intention of getting some pig feed and driving back.

It was just dumb luck that Tyler was in the back of the farm stand with a clipboard. As she walked up she noticed he was documenting every item in the stand.

"Excuse me." She paused in front of the stand and waited for Tyler to finish counting. He cleared his throat then looked over at her.

"Oh, I'm sorry, I didn't see you there. Have you been waiting long?"

"No, just a moment or two. I'm here to take advantage of your sale on pig feed."

"Oh, it's a great one. We have the big bags on sale as well."

"I see that. I'll take one of those." She handed him the money for the large package and smiled. "Is Zac around to help me get it into the trunk?" She groaned. "I'm not sure I'm strong enough to lift it in myself."

She watched Tyler's reaction closely. He froze when she mentioned Zac's name. He turned back to face her.

"Who?" He narrowed his eyes.

"Zac. I've seen him around here on the farm. Isn't he a farmhand?" She looked past him towards the barn.

"Not for me he's not. If you give me a minute I'll help you with it."

"Are you sure? I know I've seen him here a few

times. In fact, I think I've seen him talking directly to you." Ally embellished the truth to try to get more information out of him.

"I think you're mistaken. I don't have anyone on my staff named Zac." He sighed and turned around fully to face her. "If you're talking about the kid that keeps hounding me for a job, no he doesn't work for me. He's always hanging around here hoping for me to hire him."

"Why don't you?" Ally kept her voice casual, as if she was just maintaining the conversation.

"I don't have anything against the kid really, but he works for Bob, and he was always hanging around Nigel. I don't know, there's just something off about him. I don't hire anyone that I don't trust. There have been some strange things happening around here lately. I can't be too cautious."

"That makes sense." She lingered for a moment. She wanted to ask him more questions, but she remembered Luke's advice to be careful. "I guess he must be working for a different farm too then."

"A farm other than Bob's?" Tyler looked up and narrowed his eyes.

"He has to be working somewhere else to be flashing the kind of cash that he has on him." She shook her head. "I assumed he was moonlighting on your farm, but I guess not."

"No, definitely not. Here, let me get this." He grunted as he hefted the bag up off the ground and carried it towards the car. Ally popped the trunk. "I stapled your receipt to the bag. The sale is on until next Monday if you want to stock up." He dropped it down into the trunk.

"Thanks." She nodded at Tyler. He tipped his hat to her then walked back to the farm stand. Ally closed the trunk and climbed into the car. Why was Tyler so suspicious of Zac's intentions?

Chapter Ten

On a hunch Ally decided to stop by the flower shop again to talk to Tracy. Maybe she could give her some information about Zac. She hoped she might know if there was anything further to what Tyler had said about Zac's involvement with him. She parked outside the flower shop and headed inside the shop. When she opened the door to the shop she was greeted by an empty room. There were plenty of bouquets scattered around, along with other trinkets, but there was no one behind the counter. She walked up to the counter and peeked past it.

Though she could see a few shelves and a storage area, she still didn't see anyone who might work there. As she started to turn away she heard raised voices just outside the side door. She moved a little closer to it so that she could make out what was being said. She peered around the door frame and she could see that Tracy Flowers was talking to a tall, older man. His face was red with anger.

"I checked three times. I don't play around with that pesticide, and you know it. You are the only other person that has access to it. So, how is there so much missing, Tracy?"

Tracy shied back from him. "I don't know what you're talking about. You must have miscounted. Why would I want anything to do with something like that?"

"I don't know why, but I do know that it is missing, and because of that I think that you must have taken it. I know I didn't take it. So what am I supposed to think, Tracy?"

"You need to stop accusing me of things. You're being crazy. It's a pesticide, I don't even have my own garden!"

"Don't play dumb with me, Tracy. When I hired you I told you what that stuff was capable of, that's why every bag had to be signed in and out and its use had to be documented. Now I have bags that weren't signed out, that are missing and can't be found. If you don't tell me what you did with them, I'm going to have to report this to the police."

"No, you can't do that!"

"What else can I do, Tracy?" He narrowed his eyes. "Whatever you've done, I don't want it coming back on me. I really thought you were better than this." He shook his head.

"Please, you can't go to the police. I'll do anything you ask me to do. Just don't call them."

He stared at her hard. Ally thought he might even strike her, but instead he hung his head.

"I will give you three hours to return the bags or tell me where they are, after that I'm going to the police. That's it. That's your last chance. Understand?"

Ally's eyes widened as she heard Tracy begin to cry. She knew Tracy was saying something, but her voice was too muffled for Ally to hear. Ally saw the man start to walk towards her so she stepped back from the door. A moment later the man who she presumed was the owner of the shop burst through the door. He pushed it with such force that Ally had to jump further back from it before it collided with her. His face was coated in sweat, and he barely looked at Ally. It was easy to see that he was quite disturbed. She backed away a few more steps, and bumped into one of the displays. He looked up at the sound of the items as they knocked together. He paused when he saw her.

"Oh, I'm sorry. I didn't realize we had a customer. Did you need help with anything?"

"No thank you, sorry. I was just looking." Ally didn't stick around to have a discussion with him. She was just in time to nearly run into Tracy who was headed to the car parked in front of Ally's.

"Excuse me." She sniffled and continued past.

"Tracy? Are you okay?" Ally touched her arm. Tracy turned to look at her. She blinked, then seemed to recognize who Ally was.

"What do you care?" She narrowed her eyes. "Everyone is out to get me. First you accuse me of murder, now my boss is accusing me of theft."

"I think that you need to come clean if you're involved in this somehow, Tracy."

"I'm not involved in Nigel's death. I just did it for some money. I had no idea what Zac was doing." She wiped at her eyes and shook her head. "I have to go." She climbed into her car without another word.

Ally got behind the wheel of her car and watched as Tracy pulled out of her parking space. After a few seconds Ally followed after her. She wanted to know where Tracy planned to go and what she planned to do. As she trailed Tracy's car, Ally's cell phone began to ring. She ignored it as she was afraid she might lose track of Tracy. After three more turns Tracy began to slow down. Ally turned down a side street just in case Tracy spotted her. She drove around the block and saw that Tracy had parked in front of one of the duplexes on the street. She parked several spaces away. For some time she watched the car and the duplex. Then she remembered the phone call. She checked it to see that it was her grandmother who had called.

Ally considered calling her back, but she wanted to check out who Tracy was meeting. She walked quietly up to the duplex, then crept around the corner. The quiet sounds of a neighborhood getting ready for the evening filtered through her thoughts. Car doors slammed, and kids were called. She doubted that anyone would notice her spying. There was one small window not far from the corner. When she peered through the glass she could see Tracy and Zac. They were close enough to the window that she could hear them, too. Ally crouched down in front of the window so that she could just see inside and listened close.

"I need the rest of it back, Zac. I need it now."

"I think you need to calm down. Did you tell him that you were the one that took it?"

"No, he doesn't know for sure. You told me that we could get away with this. That no one would even know if it was missing. You said that we would never be caught."

"Yeah, well it didn't work out that way did it?"

"Why?" Tracy lunged at him. "What happened to Nigel, Zac? What did you do to him?"

Zac grabbed her by the shoulders and snapped her body back and forth. "You're acting crazy. No one knows that you did anything. If you just keep your mouth shut everything will be fine."

"No, I don't want anything to do with this anymore. I want the poison back. I want to make sure that it is accounted for, now." She flinched. Ally assumed that Zac might have squeezed her shoulders too hard.

"Are you nuts? You want to go to jail for this? He'll have us both arrested. Then what? Nigel isn't here to pay for our lawyers."

"You did this. You pulled me into all of this. You said you had forgotten to place Bob's order on time. That you just needed to use it until the order came in and then you would replace it. But you never planned to, did you?"

"You are just as involved in this as I am, I didn't see you turn down the money."

"What did you do with the poison, Zac? Is that why Nigel got hurt?" Tracy's eyes widened at the realization.

"Don't talk about that here. In fact don't talk about it at all."

"This is nuts, not me. I never agreed to any of this. No one was ever supposed to get hurt."

"You better keep your mouth shut or you're going to be the next one that gets hurt." He stared into her eyes. "You understand?"

"All right, all right. I understand. I won't tell anyone anything." Her voice shifted from enraged to fearful.

"You need to do more than that. You need to make yourself scarce for a while. It's time that you let this all die down. I can't trust you to keep quiet. So whatever you have to do to get out of town, you just need to do it."

"Won't that make me look even more guilty to

my boss?"

"You are guilty, aren't you?" He moved closer to her until she was pinned back against the front door. "You want to act like you're so innocent in all of this, but the truth is that you are the one who let me take it, aren't you?" He poked a finger hard into her shoulder. "Before you try to cry victim in all of this remember that you are guilty. No one forced you to do what you did."

"But you told me it was because you had stuffed up the order. I needed the money. You lied to me."

"It doesn't matter. It won't matter to your boss, and it won't matter to a jury. If my boss heard you saying any of this, then he would have me handle things differently. You need to get out of town before he finds out."

"I can't believe this." Tracy shook her head. "This is like a nightmare."

"Yeah well, trust me, you're not going to wake up. So do what I say, understand?"

"Yes." She sighed. "Yes Zac, I understand."

He pushed her away from the door and stepped through it. Ally flattened herself against the side of the house. When she heard the front door slam shut she held her breath. If Zac decided to walk around the side of the house she would have nowhere to hide. A few moments later the roar of an engine assured her that he chose to go to his car instead.

Ally lingered for a few more minutes. When she peeked inside the window, she didn't see anyone inside. She presumed that Tracy had left. She took a deep breath, then stepped around the side of the house. She was about to walk to her car when the door to the duplex opened. Tracy stepped out and bumped into Ally's shoulder. She gasped and spun around. "What are you doing here?"

"I was just in the area." Ally's eyes widened. She was too flustered to come up with another explanation.

"That's not true. Were you following me?"

She glared at her. "What did you hear?"

"Nothing."

"Don't lie."

"Okay, I heard arguing, and I wanted to make sure that you were okay."

"I'm fine. Can't you tell?" She shook her head. "You're nosy. Possibly the nosiest person that I have ever met. I wish you had never found out about me and Nigel. You need to leave me alone."

"Tracy, I'm just trying to figure out what happened to Nigel. From what I heard I think you would like to know the same thing."

"If you know what's best for you, you'll forget everything you heard." Tracy glared into her eyes. "You have no idea what you're getting yourself involved in."

"Maybe not, but I know that running isn't the answer." Ally tried to block Tracy's way to her car. "Tracy, just think about it. You need to find a way out of this. I have a friend that is a police officer. He can help if you let him."

Tracy pushed past her. "Forget you ever saw me!" She rushed to her car and was gone a minute later. Ally stared after her debating with herself what to do. She wasn't sure if she should follow her. Luke's warnings played through her mind which was accompanied by the feeling that there was something at the shop she was forgetting. She got so caught up in the investigation that she hadn't been paying much attention to the needs of the shop. She decided she was better off checking on things there first. That would give her some time to piece together what she knew.

Chapter Eleven

As Ally pulled into the parking lot of the shop her phone beeped with a text from her grandmother.

Have you decided to go with Luke to the dance? I can get you both tickets. They are selling fast.

Ally smiled to herself. Her grandmother was not going to let the idea go. Still, the more she thought about it, the more she was certain she would enjoy it. She sent a quick text in return.

Go ahead and get the tickets. Thanks!

A buzz of excitement rushed through her at the thought. It made her nervous to think of going on an actual date with Luke, but she also couldn't wait to see what would happen. She only hoped that she wouldn't end up injuring one of his feet. Her grandmother texted back.

Yay!

Ally smiled as she climbed out of the car and headed towards the front of the shop. After a quick glance around to make sure everything was in place she pulled out her keys. She turned the key in the lock and pushed the door open.

Once inside the familiar scents of the shop soothed her nerves. Yes, there was a lot going on, but she was back at the shop in familiar surroundings, and the investigation could wait while she tended to the shop. As she walked away from the door towards the cash register, the bell above it rang. She had forgotten to lock the door behind her. She turned to see Colin step inside. "Ally? I need to talk to you."

"Colin, what are you doing here?" Ally studied

him. She could see the tension in the crease of his brow and the way he curled his hands into fists.

"I wanted to talk to you. I came by earlier, but your grandmother said that you were out. I need to know if you found anything that might help clear my name. My lawyer said it's only a matter of time before the police arrest me. This is like a nightmare." He looked into her eyes. "I know you probably don't want me coming to the shop, but I'm desperate."

"Colin, I understand why you're upset. Why don't you take a seat? I'll get you coffee and chocolate." She guided him towards one of the tables and started to walk into the back.

"Ally, thank you, but no, I really don't have time for this. I keep thinking back to the last time I saw my brother. I know he wanted to tell me something, but I have no idea what it was." He shook his head and groaned with frustration. "All of this is just so much to take in. I don't want to end up in jail and never find out what Nigel was trying to tell me."

"I think I am starting to work out what your brother wanted to tell you."

"What?" He leaned closer to her.

"I can't tell you, not yet." Ally cringed as he narrowed his eyes.

"I thought you were helping me out with this. If you can't tell me the information that you've found, who can you tell?"

"I just don't want you doing anything rash. I want to be sure I have the right information before I pass anything onto you."

"That's not your decision. This is my brother we're talking about. Whatever it was that he wanted me to know, I want you to tell me."

"You have to trust me on this, Colin. I am going to get to the bottom of all of this. Just give me a little time to get there."

"How much more time?" Colin frowned. He sighed and shook his head. "I'm sorry, I know that none of this is your responsibility. I'm grateful that you're on my side. I'm just frustrated. To lose my brother and be suspected of his murder at the same time is ripping me apart."

"Of course it is." Ally rubbed her hand across his shoulder and leaned in closer to him. "I know you didn't do it, Colin."

"Do you?" He met her eyes. "Or am I still a suspect in your eyes?"

"Ally?" Luke pushed the door open and stepped inside. "Everything okay?" Ally drew back from Colin and nodded.

"Have you two met?" Ally asked.

"No," Luke said while Colin shook his head.

"Colin Dean this is my friend Detective Luke Elm," Ally explained as they shook hands. "Colin just stopped by to see if I had heard anything about his brother's murder."

"Oh." Luke looked at Colin. "I'm from Blue River so I'm not on the case, but from what I hear the Mainbry police are getting closer."

"Right. Is that closer to the truth or closer to my arrest?" Colin said tensely and stared at Luke.

"The truth, I'm sure." Ally moved between them. "I am learning more and more as quickly as I can."

"Okay, if you say so. I don't like that you're hiding information from me." Colin furrowed a brow. "I might be able to help."

"The most I can tell you is that I think the person involved in killing Nigel might be the same person involved in poisoning your father's crops." Ally looked over at Luke. "I have a pretty good hunch that is the case."

"What about the person?" Colin crossed his arms. "Who do you think that is?"

"I can't say just yet until I get some final information," Ally said. "Just be a little more patient."

"I'm trying to be, but I'm tempted to catch the next flight out of the country."

"Don't do that." Luke moved past Ally towards Colin. "If you run you'll look guilty."

"I guess you would know. Are you going to tell

your buddies I'm a flight risk now?" He stared at Luke.

"Like I said I have nothing to do with the case. But you should be careful who you say that to," Luke said.

"Is that a threat?" Colin stepped towards Luke. Luke held up his hands.

"Not at all. I'm just trying to offer you some advice. There's nothing that makes a suspect look more guilty than running."

"See, I'm a suspect to him, too." Colin sighed. "Just keep me up to date, Ally, please."

"I will." She walked him to the door of the shop. "We're going to get this cleared up." She patted his arm, but he pulled away and gave her a skeptical shake of his head. She closed the door and turned to face Luke. With every ounce of willpower she had she ignored the fact that he looked incredibly handsome as he leaned up against the counter and stared across the room at her. "What was that about?" Ally asked.

"What?"

"The whole speech about looking guilty."

"I just told him the truth." Luke straightened up and continued to study her. "If he takes off like that, he's going to get caught, and the consequences are going to be huge."

"But you're acting like he's guilty when he hasn't even been arrested."

"I am not, I just know that if he runs he will look very guilty. I also think that he might be arrested. I think it's just a matter of time. Unless there's something you need to tell me." He crossed the distance between them. "Did you find anything further?"

"Yes actually. I found out that Tracy and Zac stole pesticide from the flower shop. Tracy didn't seem to know what it would be used for." Ally pursed her lips. "I'm just not sure who the mastermind behind that is. If it's Zac or someone else calling the shots."

"That's strange. Wouldn't Bob's farm have

some on hand?" Luke rubbed his eyes. "Why would Zac go to the trouble of stealing it?"

"Maybe, but Bob would notice if some went missing, wouldn't he." Ally studied him for a moment. She could see his exhaustion reflected in the droop of his lips and the dark circles under his eyes.

"What do you think they used it for?"

"Remember, Bob's crops have been mysteriously dying." She frowned.

"Yes, I do remember that. You think they were poisoning his crops? But that doesn't make any sense. Zac worked for Bob." Luke brushed his hand back through his hair and blinked. "Where is the connection?"

"I'm not sure, yet, but I know it involved Nigel."

"It certainly seems so."

"When I asked Tyler about Zac all he said was that he was trying to get a job from him." Ally touched his shoulder. "Are you okay? You look like you need some rest." Luke shrugged.

"I haven't gotten much sleep, but I'm fine. If Zac got such a bump up in pay at Bob's farm after Nigel left, why would Zac want to take a job for less pay at Tyler's?" Luke narrowed his eyes. "Wait a minute. You talked to Tyler?"

Ally cringed. "Well, just for a minute or two."

"Ally, I asked you not to."

"I know, and I wouldn't have. But Arnold was starving."

"So, you're blaming this on Arnold?" He grinned. "That's a new one."

"I had to get him some pig feed and Tyler is having a sale." She tilted her head to the side. "Totally innocent."

"Sure, except I asked you not to." He locked eyes with her.

"I was careful."

"Hm." Luke shoved his hands into his pockets. "Why does it seem like that's only because the opportunity for danger didn't come up?"

"Luke, I just bought some pig food." Ally shrugged. "Colin's freedom and reputation hang in the balance here. If he gets arrested for this murder that's something that he will never forget and neither will this town."

"Let's hope it's solved before that happens."

"I have an idea."

"What are you thinking?" Luke asked.

"Someone said Zac has been flashing cash around. I want to find out where the money was coming from. For Zac to get involved in all of this, someone must have been putting him up to it."

"Maybe." Luke rubbed his chin.

"What, you think it's something different?"

"Well, this case stinks of sibling rivalry."

"But Colin didn't do it." Ally narrowed her eyes.

"I agree. I could be wrong, but I don't think he did kill Nigel. I think we need to consider that he might not be the only sibling though."

"What do you mean?"

"I mean that Zac and Nigel were close, like brothers. It doesn't matter that they weren't related. Maybe they had a feud we didn't know about." He rubbed his eyes again.

"Oh Luke, you really need some sleep."

"I've been trying, but something's been keeping me up at night."

"What?" She met his eyes.

"Wondering if you're ever going to dance with me." He rested a hand on her hip and turned her towards him a little. "It's been driving me crazy."

"Liar." She laughed.

"Well, that and the drug sting."

"Yes, that might have a little more to do with it, don't you think?"

"Maybe." His hand lingered on her hip. "But I'd still like to know."

"I'm thinking about it." She smiled. She didn't

have the courage to say that she had already asked her grandmother to get the tickets. If she told him she was going that would mean that she was exposing herself to getting hurt and she wouldn't be able to get out of it if she changed her mind.

"Don't take too long, I need time to buy a suit."

"Don't worry, like I said, I'm still thinking about it and I'll let you know in plenty of time," Ally said. "Now you should go home and take a nap, hm?"

He nodded and leaned away as he yawned. "That might be a good idea." He glanced at his watch. "I should be able to catch a few hours. But try to behave, hm?"

"Oh wow, you really don't know me very well." She laughed. He winked at her then headed out of the shop.

Chapter Twelve

After Luke left Ally looked through the recent orders. Something had been nagging at the back of her mind. Just as she suspected there was an order that was due to be delivered. Ally had about fifteen minutes to put together a box of chocolates and get out the door. She tossed in a bag of cookies as a bonus. With a sense of relief she headed for the van. If she hadn't decided to stop in and check on things she might never have remembered the order.

Just as Ally was about to get into the van, she remembered that she had yet to feed Arnold. She decided that she would take her car instead, it wasn't too hot out and it was a small delivery. After she delivered the order, she could stop by the cottage and feed Arnold, then return to the shop to make sure everything was shut down correctly.

Ally climbed into the driver's seat. Before she started the engine she sent a text to her grandmother. She wanted to let her know that she was making the delivery so she would know where she was in case she went to the cottage to walk Arnold, like she often did. She didn't want her grandmother to worry about a very hungry pig. She drove towards the address on the delivery slip.

Ally parked the car in front of the house and carried the package up to the door. She knocked, then glanced around as she waited for someone to answer. When a woman answered the door Ally smiled at her.

"Delivery from Charlotte's." Ally held out the box.

"Oh wonderful. Thank you. What great service." She handed Ally a few dollars. "For you dear. Thanks again." Ally smiled as she accepted the tip.

"Thank you. Enjoy!"

As she walked back to the car it crossed her mind that she was close to the farms. It wouldn't hurt to take a drive over there and see if Zac was at either farm. After his encounter with Tracy he was likely eager to get the situation with the pesticide resolved. That meant that he might have gone to whoever was paying him so well to poison the crops. She decided to take a spin around both farms just to see what was happening. She didn't even intend to get out of the car.

As Ally drove towards the farms she sorted through what she knew so far. There was no question in her mind that Zac was involved in the murder. But was he the killer? And who was the person actually calling the shots. It had to be someone that had the power and wealth to tempt Zac into betraying his boss. Or was it Bob all along? She couldn't think of a good reason that Bob would want to poison his own crops.

Unless, it was his way of trying to draw Nigel back. Her eyes widened at the thought. Yes, that was very possible. Maybe Bob thought that if Nigel saw the farm was in trouble, he would come back home. She shook her head. But that would only work if Bob actually wanted to reconcile with his son. He didn't exactly seem like a grieving father to her.

She flipped on the radio and sat back for the drive to the farm. As she approached Bob's farm she noticed that a large portion of the crops were wilted. Whoever had poisoned them had been at it again the night before. She took a deep breath and decided to talk to Bob again. He might have his own suspicions about who was involved in the sabotage. As she rolled up the long driveway she noticed that the door to the barn was open. She slowed down even more. A moment later she caught sight of Zac as he stepped out of the barn. He was only out of the barn for a moment before he ducked back inside.

Ally's heart pounded. She had witnessed what kind of man Zac really was through the window of the duplex he lived in. He had put his hands on Tracy and threatened her. She was sure he'd be willing to do much worse to her. But she was willing to risk it, she was determined to find out the truth once and for all. That meant that she needed to get Zac alone. The barn was a good opportunity for her to do just that as there was only one way out. She drove the car further up the drive to the parking area. There were a few other cars parked there as well.

As Ally walked towards the barn her heart began to race. Was she taking too big of a chance by being alone with him? She walked as quietly as she could. She could see that the door to the barn was left open about two inches. When she reached it, she paused in front of the doors and peered through the crack into the barn. She watched as Zac began moving the bales of hay from one side of the barn to the other again. He wore the same thick gloves he had on the first time she saw him do this. It still didn't make sense to her that he would move the bales of hay back and forth.

When Zac moved the last bale of hay Ally saw him crouch down. He brushed some loose hay and dirt out of the way and found a handle underneath. He lifted the handle and looked down into a small storage area. Ally's heart skipped a beat as she wondered what might be down there. She assumed it was the missing pesticide. In a slow, cautious movement Zac lifted out a medium sized white bag. She was sure it was the same pesticide that Tracy and her boss had fought about. With the bag in his hand he seemed much more threatening to her. She had no idea what it could do, but she guessed that it was rather dangerous if it needed to be monitored so closely. He set the bag down on the floor of the barn, then put his phone to his ear.

"Are you here?" He paused. "Yes, I'm ready. When are you going to be here? It's almost dark." He paused again and looked up at the ceiling of the barn. "That's fine but don't take forever. We only have a small window." He turned towards the doors of the barn. Ally ducked back fast. She hoped that she had moved fast enough to avoid being spotted by Zac, but she couldn't be sure.

Ally hurried back to her car. As soon as she got to it she saw a small black truck pull into the driveway. She ducked down beside her car as the headlights flashed past her. She watched as the truck disappeared behind the barn. Whoever it was she was sure they were there to meet with Zac. This might be her only opportunity to try to find out the truth about what was happening between the two farms and hopefully who the murderer was.

Ally saw a man walk around to the entrance of the barn. It was too dark to make him out clearly. He went inside the barn. She thought about going back to the doors to listen in, but that might be too big of a risk. Instead she decided to watch for some time to see what the two men would do. Not long after, two figures stepped out of the barn. From a distance she recognized the taller figure as Zac, but she couldn't make out who the other figure was. Zac carried something in his hands. It looked like the bag of poison.

As Ally watched they walked towards the fields. Ally had to think fast. She wanted to follow them but she didn't know the land. She was afraid that she would get lost. She needed some kind of trail that she could follow to find her way back to her car. She opened the trunk and quickly cut the bag of pig feed open with her key. She scooped a large amount of pig feed into her pockets. Then she began to follow them at a safe distance. She dropped a sprinkling of the pig feed behind her as she entered the fields. The two men were quiet, but she could hear the shuffle of their feet. They walked for quite some time before they stopped.

"Here's a good spot." The voice was muffled, and belonged to the other man. She tried to work out who the voice belonged to, but she couldn't. Maybe she was mistaken but she thought she had heard it recently. "Make sure you lay it on thick, none of this should survive."

"Are you sure you want to do this? That's a lot of crops to destroy," Zac asked.

"Do I pay you to ask me questions?" The man growled.

"No, Sir. But, I think you're taking this too far."

"I also don't pay you to think. Do as I say or I

will get someone else to do it. Understand?"

"Yeah, I understand." He paused. Ally heard the shuffle of feet and the subtle whoosh of something poured out of a bag. "There."

"Hey, watch it. You should have waited until I was further away," the man complained.

"I just did what you said."

"Do we have a problem here, Zac?" The tone of the man's voice deepened. "If you're ready to jump ship you need to tell me now."

"Where would I go?" Zac sighed. "It was harder than I thought, with Nigel. I thought he would be okay with everything. Thankful even. " Ally froze. Did Zac just admit to killing Nigel?

"You did the right thing."

"Maybe. But it doesn't feel that way."

"You came to me, Zac, don't forget that. You didn't want to be a nobody for the rest of your life. Nigel proved he wasn't really your friend when he was going to turn you in. Where was his loyalty?"

"You're right." The sound of Zac's cough

shattered the hush of the field around them. "Let's get this done."

"All right. Keep at it."

Ally heard the shuffle of feet again. As she started to back away to ensure that neither of them would see her, she stepped back on something slippery. She bit into her bottom lip to keep from crying out as she struggled to keep her balance. With a stumble forward she had to grab onto some of the stalks around her. She steadied herself, but knew she had made far too much noise in the process. She froze as everything became very silent. She couldn't tell where the two men were. Her heart pounded so hard that she was sure they could hear it thumping. She closed her eyes in an attempt to calm her mind. As she listened she heard a subtle snap and crunch a few steps behind her. Ice flowed through her veins. She was too scared to even turn and look.

Chapter Thirteen

Charlotte paced back and forth through the empty parking spot that Ally's car should have been parked in. Arnold paced back and forth right behind her. She had already called the customer who ordered the delivery to confirm that it had been received. Ally should have been back in ten or fifteen minutes. Instead nearly an hour had slipped by. It wasn't like Ally not to give her an idea of when she intended to be back if she was going to be late.

The sun started to set, and despite multiple calls and texts Ally hadn't responded. At the rumble of an engine Charlotte looked up expectantly. However, it was just a delivery truck that rumbled past. Charlotte's heart skipped a beat, she knew that something wasn't right. After many years of experience she learned not to ignore her instincts. Without hesitation she dialed Luke's number. He would either know where Ally was or he would help to find her. He answered after one ring.

"Charlotte, is everything okay?" He sounded anxious the moment that he answered the phone. Charlotte assumed that he knew if she was calling, there was probably a problem.

"Luke, I'm sorry to bother you, I'm probably being silly, but have you heard from Ally?"

"Not since this afternoon. Did something happen?"

"Well, she's late back from a delivery. She's not at the shop. She's not answering my texts or calls. I'm just a little worried."

"That's not like Ally at all." He paused. "I have an idea of where she might have gone."

"You do? Where?"

"Oh no, I'm not falling for that one. You stay at the shop, I will come and get you."

"I have Arnold."

"That's fine, there's room in the car. Don't you move a muscle. I don't want to lose track of both of you in the same day."

"All right, but hurry, Luke. Now, I'm really worried."

After Luke hung up the phone Charlotte's attention returned to the pig. He still ran around in circles. He snorted like wild. Charlotte crouched down and patted the top of his head.

"It's all right, Arnold, I know you're worried, I am too. But we're going to find Ally and she will be just fine."

Arnold snorted again. He nuzzled her hand, but didn't seem convinced. Charlotte frowned. "Yes, I know. I'm worried, too," she repeated.

***

Ally started to turn to see who was behind her. She felt the pain in her head before she even recognized that anyone had struck her. As the pain burned through her head, her knees buckled then she hit the ground. The last thing she was aware of, were hands wrapped tight around her ankles and the sensation of being pulled. When she woke what felt like only a second later, her head ached so much that she couldn't open her

189

eyes. After struggling for a few minutes she managed to force them apart.

It took her a while to process where she was. There was still dirt under her, but there was also a roof above her. Her head ached bad enough that she could guess someone had hit her very hard. From what she could tell she was alone in what she assumed was the barn. As she tried to struggle to her feet she discovered that her hands and ankles were tied. Her heart dropped. There was no way she could escape. She couldn't crawl. The ropes were tied too tight for her to work her way out. To make things even worse, she had left her cell phone in the car.

After panic flooded her, she tried to bring herself back to a calm state. She knew for sure she wasn't going to be able to get out of the situation if she didn't have her wits about her. Instead, what she needed to do was find a solution. There had to be one. She did her best to look around the barn, though it was quite dark. A bit of evening light filtered in from the partially open barn doors. Was it Zac that had struck her? Or his partner? She had no idea, but she could hear voices from outside. The conversation was a tense one filled with hissed words and sharp retorts. One voice was Zac's. She still couldn't work out who the other man was.

"I don't know if I can do this." Zac's voice trembled.

"Sure you can. I killed Nigel, now it's your turn. You even dealt with your best friend's body for me. Don't wuss out on me now, all right?" Ally held her breath as she listened to the confession.

"This is different, and you know it. I am not a murderer. There's no way I can do this. Plus, people will find out. She's practically dating that cop, remember?"

"I don't care who she is dating. There is only one option here. It has to be done."

"I can't do it. Why can't you do it?"

"Why can't I do it?" The other man's voice raised. "Because I am not a criminal, Zac. That's why I hired you. I had to kill Nigel because you lost your nerve. I had no choice but I'm not killing another person. If I was a criminal, I would have put Nigel's body in the wheelbarrow and taken care of it myself. Then you would be out of all that cash you enjoy so much. I doubt you would enjoy that too much. Would you?"

"No. I just think this is over the line. I mean, she's a girl."

"Oh, is that it?" He laughed. "Fine, if you're so worried about killing a girl, then just do it in an easier way."

"How?"

"Just slip her some of the poison, it'll be over fast, then get rid of the body."

"I can't do that." Zac's voice raised. "That poison isn't going to just kill her. It's horrible stuff. She'll be screaming."

"That's what duct tape is for."

"I won't do that. I can't."

"Just what I need, a criminal who has grown

a conscience. I don't care how you kill her, just get it done."

"There has to be some other way."

"There sure is. If you don't kill her, I will, and you along with her. I only work with people who are loyal to me. I don't want to deal with some kid that's decided to go soft on me. So either you prove your worth to me, or you're just as much a liability."

"All right, I will. I will. But not like that. Not with poison."

"Fine, fine, if you're so concerned about her suffering then find another way to do it. But stop fussing about it. Just do it quick and quiet."

"Why can't we just let her go? We don't even know if she knows anything."

"And if she does? Are you ready to go to jail for the rest of your life, Zac? You will go down for not only poisoning the crops, but Nigel's murder as well. I certainly won't be going down for it. I'm not willing to risk letting her go in case she knows something. If you are willing to risk it, then that is a problem."

"I'm not. I'll take care of it."

"Remember. Make it quick and quiet. Understand?"

"Yes."

"Zac, I'm trusting you on this. Don't make me regret that."

Ally heard the creek of the barn door. Her heart pounded as she looked around again for an escape. There was a high window, but she didn't think there was any way for her to get to that. There was a small door where hay could be shoveled in or out, but it was all the way on the other side of the barn and closed. With her hands and feet bound there was no way for her to even find a way to hide. As she watched the barn door open she opened her mouth to scream. As the sound poured out of her mouth Zac rushed forward with wide eyes.

"Why are you awake?" He clamped a hand

over her mouth and cringed. Ally tried to fight him but he easily held her still.

"I said quiet!" The voice from outside the barn was filled with frustration. Ally knew the more she fought, the more she would speed up her death. Whoever was outside was pulling the strings and he didn't want to hear a sound. She settled down and looked into Zac's eyes. He relaxed a little when she stopped fighting.

"Just be quiet, okay?"

She nodded and widened her eyes. When he drew his hand away from her mouth she struggled to stay calm. He paced back and forth as if he was trying to decide what his next move would be. Ally watched him move. At one time she might have believed that he was a good person and that she had a chance. But now that she knew that he was involved in the murder and what he was capable of, she also knew just how much danger she was in.

Chapter Fourteen

Charlotte looked up and down the road again. She checked her watch.

"Where are you, Luke?"

As if to answer her question she saw his car turn a corner and drive towards the shop. Charlotte stepped back on the sidewalk and held tight onto Arnold's leash. Luke's car pulled up to the sidewalk in front of the shop. Charlotte opened the back door and Arnold hopped in. She closed the door and climbed into the front seat. Arnold snorted and rubbed his nose across the window.

"So you know where she might be?" Charlotte snapped her seatbelt into place.

"Oh, I have an idea. I hope I'm not right, but I certainly have an idea." His eyes narrowed as he gripped the wheel tight. Charlotte frowned as she noticed how tense he was.

"It's all right, Luke. She's going to be fine."

"I hope so," he muttered and applied the brakes at a stop sign. He turned in the direction of the farms. "What I can't understand is why she just won't trust me and tell me what she's up to."

"It's easy for some people to trust, Luke. The ones who struggle with it, are the ones who have been hurt and still have some healing to do. Ally prides herself on being independent." Charlotte looked over at him. "She acts before she thinks sometimes and she is very curious. That's why she gets herself into some messes. But she always has good intentions."

"I get that. I just worry that her good intentions will land her in a situation she can't escape." He sped up as he approached the road that led to the farms.

"That's what we're for, dear." Charlotte patted his arm. "Just in case."

He smiled as he glanced over at her. The smile faded the moment that he pulled into the driveway that led to Tyler's farm. He scanned all of the vehicles in the parking area and up near the house. None was Ally's car. His heart dropped. When he turned around, his headlights trailed across the barn.

There was no sign of anyone inside.

"Maybe we should walk the property. Maybe she hid the car somewhere." Luke put the car in park.

"No." Charlotte narrowed her eyes. "No, she isn't here, Luke."

"Are you sure? She mentioned she might go to talk to Tyler again."

"My gut is telling me we're not in the right place. Trust me, Luke." She put the car back into drive. "Let's go."

Luke took control of the car and drove back down the road. He looked anxiously out the window as they drove past the fields between Tyler and Bob's farms. It was easy to see when the property shifted because many of Bob's crops were wilted. He turned the car up the driveway that led to Bob's farm. As he approached he noticed that there were a few cars in the parking area.

"There it is!" Charlotte gasped. "Ally's car!"

Luke aimed the headlights at the front of the car. There was no one in the driver's seat. Charlotte hopped out of the car with the spare set of keys. Arnold climbed right into the front seat and jumped out behind her. She ignored his snorts as she fumbled with the keys. Her hand trembled as she opened the door.

"I'm going to call her phone again." Luke pulled out his cell phone.

"Don't bother." Charlotte shook her head. "It's here." Charlotte picked up Ally's cell phone out of the console between the seats.

"Oh no." Luke frowned and glanced around the property. "Where did she go?"

"Arnold?" Charlotte glanced around. "Arnold, get back here!" Arnold headed for a nearby field. He snorted and snapped up something that was on the ground. "Arnold!"

"Wait." Luke stepped forward. He followed after the pig and shined his flashlight on what was on the ground. "That's strange. What is this on the ground?" Charlotte followed the path of the flashlight beam.

"That's pig food."

"Why would that be here? Does Bob have pigs?"

"No, he doesn't. But Ally was supposed to pick up some pig food for Arnold." She frowned and looked around again. Through the shadows of the evening light she could see a barn in the distance, but there didn't seem to be any light on. "What if she left us a trail?"

"A trail?" Luke scratched his head. "That seems a little farfetched."

"Not to me it doesn't. Ally probably realized she was getting into something she shouldn't and decided to leave the trail for us to find. It's the only reason why the food would be spread out like this."

"I don't know." Luke shook his head.

"Why don't I follow the trail and you head for the barn?" Charlotte held tight onto Arnold's leash.

"I don't think I like that idea. I don't want you out of my sight."

"I appreciate that, Luke, but I'm not under arrest, so you don't have a say about where I go. I'm going to follow this trail. You and I both know there's a better chance of finding Ally safe if we split up. The closest structure other than the house is that barn. It doesn't look like anyone's in there, but it's still worth checking out. Just like this trail is."

Luke shoved his hands in his pockets. He clenched his jaw as he looked between the two areas.

"Do you have your cell phone? Here's a flashlight."

"I'll be fine, Luke, I promise," she said as she took the flashlight from him and held up her phone. "While you were still in diapers I was, well never mind that, let's just say I can take care of myself."

He raised an eyebrow and met her gaze. "Be careful."

"I will." She smiled and patted his cheek. "You be careful, too. You have a dance to go to."

"If she says yes." He rolled his eyes.

"She did." Charlotte winked at him. "She's already bought the tickets." He stared at her for a moment, then snapped back to the reality of the situation.

"Let's go, before it gets any later." He walked off in the direction of the barn. Charlotte let Arnold lead her through the field. The further in she walked, the more concerned she became. Was Ally led out here? Was she following someone? She wanted to call out for her, but she was afraid that if someone had her, they would hear her voice and become alarmed. She needed to know where Ally was first.

They were almost to the middle of the field when Arnold began to squeal and snort. He danced around in a small circle, then tugged hard on his leash. The sudden lunge knocked Charlotte off balance. She landed hard on her bottom, and Arnold's leash whipped out of her hands. Before she could get back to her feet the pig was gone. Her hand brushed over something solid in the dirt. She shone her flashlight on the spot and discovered Ally's car keys in the soil. Her heart lurched. Ally was there. She had been in the middle of this field. Now she was gone. Charlotte got to her feet and tried to find Arnold. She could only follow him by the sounds of his snorts and squeals.

Chapter Fifteen

Ally tried to control her fear, but it was nearly impossible. Every step Zac took in his pacing back and forth reminded her that he was one moment closer to making a decision about how he was going to deal with her. She wriggled her wrists back and forth and hoped that somehow she would be able to get free. The more she wriggled, the tighter the ropes became.

"Zac." She took a risk by speaking, but the anticipation was terrible. He paused and looked over at her. "Zac, let me go. You know it's the right thing to do. You don't want to do this. Someone else is making you do it. I can help you. I can protect you."

"You can't protect me." Zac shook his head. "There's no coming back from what I've done. Nothing will change it."

"I can get you a deal. We can work something out. You didn't even kill Nigel, but if you kill me then you are a murderer. Things happen, Zac, it doesn't have to be the end of the world. You still have the power here. You can make the right decision."

"Stop, please just stop. I don't have any other choice."

"You aren't a murderer, Zac. Who killed Nigel?" She wanted to keep him talking to delay him. She also really wanted to know who the murderer was.

"Stop!" Zac shouted. "I have to do this."

He picked up a threadbare blanket from the ground and gripped it tight in his hands. She stared at the blanket and wondered if he might wrap her up in it to transport her somewhere else. Had that been the blanket that Nigel's body was wrapped in? When she looked up into Zac's eyes he looked afraid. He had no intention of transporting her anywhere. He intended to take care of things right then.

Ally drew breath after breath as her panic increased. If only she had let someone know where she was there might have been some chance that someone would look for her. But no one knew, and no one was coming. Her heart sank as she thought of all of the things she had never said to her grandmother, all of the opportunities she had missed with Luke. He walked towards her with the blanket stretched tight between his hands.

"Don't do this, Zac. You don't have to do this. I am not going to tell anyone anything. Just let me go."

"It's too late." He hung his head for a moment. "My life ended when Nigel's life did, I could have tried harder to stop it but I didn't. There is nothing left for me. If I get caught now, I'm locked up for life."

"What do you think is going to happen if you're involved in two murders?" Ally's voice cracked with desperation.

"I guess I'll find out." He leaned forward in an attempt to place the blanket over her head. Ally thrashed the best she could to try to get away from him. She managed to get her foot slammed into the toe of his boot. He yelped and jumped back, but his work boot was thick and he recovered easily. As he came back at her Ally began to scream. She knew that it was her only chance of being found.

"Don't bother. No one is going to hear you." He leaned towards her again. This time Ally swung her head upward in an attempt to head butt him. He lunged out of the way and started to come at her again. Suddenly he froze. Ally's heart pounded so loud that she barely heard the creak of the barn door. But Zac turned towards it with wide eyes. Ally held her breath as the door to the barn creaked open a little further. For a moment she held out hope that someone might be there to save her. Then she heard a very loud snort. A second later Arnold plowed into the barn and barreled straight towards Ally. He could certainly make a lot of noise. She never thought she would love the racket the pig could make, but at that moment she did.

"Where did this pig come from?" Zac dropped the blanket and lunged towards the pig. "Get out of here, you beast." He swung his foot as if he might try to kick Arnold. Ally shrieked and swung her body towards his leg just in time to deflect his kick. It hit her shin instead. Zac lost his balance as a result of the unexpected strike. He stumbled back. Arnold circled around him, and in a move he learned from Peaches he wound around and through Zac's legs. Zac grunted and fell backwards. When he struck the ground Ally thought she might be able to kick him. She swung her feet, but he rolled out of the way before she could strike him. Arnold snorted and squealed wildly. It occurred to Ally that the man outside the door who had been so worried about noise didn't seem to be bothered by the commotion Arnold was making.

"What is going on in here?" The barn door pushed open again. Ally's eyes widened as she saw Bob walk into the barn. Just before he was all the way inside Zac jumped behind the bales of hay.

Bob squinted in the dim lighting. "What is that pig doing in here?" He took a few steps forward. Ally tried to get free of the ropes. Now that she saw Bob in the barn she was sure that he had been the one talking to Zac. She was sure that Bob had killed his own son and would finish her off.

"Let me go, just let me go."

"Huh?" Bob stepped further into the barn. "You're that nosy girl, aren't you? What the heck happened to you?" He hurried over to her. "Who did this to you?"

Ally glared up at him. "As if you don't know!"

"What?" He reached for the ropes on her hands.

"Don't!" Ally drew back in fear.

"What is your problem? Are you crazy or something? I'm trying to help you here you know? Or did you want to stay tied up?"

Ally stared at him. "You really aren't involved?"

"Involved in what? Tying you up. Of course

not. I came down here looking for Zac. I thought I saw him come in here. Then I found you. So, are you going to let me untie you?"

Ally held out her hands. Her heart pounded as she hoped that she wasn't making a mistake. Just as Bob untied her hands the barn door was shoved open again. Ally didn't have a chance to see who it was before Bob was tackled to the ground. Arnold continued to squeal and snort at the bales of hay that Zac hid behind. Ally saw through the dust and dirt that Luke wrestled with Bob on the ground. But if Bob was trying to untie her, and Zac was hiding from him, then who was the person that actually hired Zac and killed Nigel? In a daze for a moment she watched as Luke pinned Bob down. He reached for the gun in his holster.

"Luke, wait, Luke!" She tugged at the ropes around her ankles in an attempt to be completely free. "It's not him, Luke. It's Zac, he's hiding!" Before she could get the ropes loose, Zac jumped out from behind the bales of hay. He held a bag of the poison in his trembling hands.

"Let me walk out of here, or everybody is going to end up in the hospital." He stared at Ally. Luke pinned Bob to the ground.

"Let me go! What is going on here! This is outrageous!" Bob flailed in Luke's grasp. Luke's expression fluctuated between concerned and confused.

"Ally?" Luke looked over at her just as she freed herself.

"Don't move, Luke. That is the poison that has been killing Bob's crops. I don't think Bob had anything to do with any of this." Luke loosened his grip on Bob, but still remained close to him. His eyes locked on Zac and the bag of poison that he held.

"What?" Bob stared at Zac. "Zac, you're the one that's been killing the crops?"

"Let him up, Luke. I don't think he's involved in any of this. The person that hired Zac killed Nigel." Ally brushed herself off. She grabbed onto Arnold's collar and kept him close. "Zac, you're going too far here."

"No, I have to get out of here. If any of you come near me you'll get a face full of this poison. Is that what you want? You might survive, but you'll wish that you didn't."

Luke moved slowly to his feet and backed away a few steps. Bob got to his feet as well with a few groans of pain from being tackled. Instead of backing away, he turned and glared at Zac.

"What are you yammering on about, Zac? You're not going to hurt anyone. Stop this nonsense and put down that bag."

"Bob, don't." Ally met his eyes. "Zac is a very dangerous man."

"Ha." Bob shook his head. "I don't believe it. He's just a kid. I don't understand what has happened here, but I know that Zac is harmless."

"I'm sorry, but that's not true." Ally moved closer to Bob. "He was involved in Nigel's murder."

"What?" Bob's eyes widened.

"Keep quiet! I didn't kill him! I couldn't!" Zac

looked towards the barn doors.

"He's not there, Zac. He's left you here alone to deal with all of this. He's not going to come back. There's no one to give you any more orders." Ally glanced over at Luke who rested his hand on his gun. There wasn't much chance that he could use the weapon, as the moment he drew it, Zac would likely throw the poison. Ally wasn't sure if he was right about the damage that the poison could do, but she also didn't want to find out. Zac growled and stomped one of his feet.

"You don't know what you're talking about. All you do is sprout lies, and more lies. I can't take this anymore. I have to find a way out." He looked around wildly. "None of this was supposed to happen." His eyes continued to dart around the room.

"But it has." Ally tried to draw his attention back to her. "It has now, and there's no way to get out of it. The only way is to surrender. He is not even going to remember your name. You understand that don't you? He used you, Zac. This was his plan all along."

"Tyler wouldn't do that to me. He said we were in this together." Ally's eyes shone at the realization. It was Tyler calling the shots. It was Tyler that killed Nigel, and Tyler that ordered for the crops to be poisoned. Ordered Ally to be murdered.

"Tyler?" Bob snarled the name. "What does he have to do with all of this?"

"He wouldn't do that." Zac shook his head and looked at Ally.

"No, you say he wouldn't? That's rather hard to believe," Ally said. "Because he's gone isn't he? He must have run off the moment that he saw Bob coming. He knew that you wouldn't be able to kill me. He knew that you would be stuck here with a hostage or a dead body, while he skipped off to freedom. He counted on you taking the fall, Zac."

"I didn't do it. I didn't do it," Zac groaned. "No, no, no."

"You're a better person than Tyler is, but

Nigel is dead and you were involved. You can't change that. But you weren't the only one who was involved in Nigel's murder. You didn't actually kill him." She knew she was walking a dangerous line. If Zac became too emotional he might just toss the poison on all of them. If she didn't get his shock to crack, he would do whatever it took to escape and they would all pay the price.

"Good lord, Zac, Nigel called you his brother." Bob shook his head as his voice cracked with grief. "I always told him he was too much of a bleeding heart, but when it came to you, I gave him the benefit of the doubt. You grew up together. How could you do this to him?"

"No!" Zac shouted as he glared at Bob. "We did not grow up together. I grew up in his shadow. Nigel grew up with the latest and newest of everything. I grew up feeding on his scraps and goodwill. You never once let me forget that, Bob. Every time Nigel would try to include me, you would make a point that I was there as a charitable gesture. Do you know what that did to me?"

Bob's eyes narrowed to slits. "I was generous to you, my son was generous to you, and you turned around and murdered him?"

"I didn't! I couldn't!"

"But you didn't stop it, did you? Nigel got you the position and the pay that you have. He fought for that. He ensured that I would not choose anyone else to replace him. He loved you, Zac." Bob's voice wavered.

"And he was going to take it all away." Zac lowered his eyes. "When he found out the truth, that I was taking payments to poison your crops, he was going to take everything from me. But I still didn't want to kill him." Zac closed his eyes. "I was going to try to cut him into the deal. I told him I'd give him half, more than half, we could go in together. But he was furious when he found out that I was the one poisoning the crops. When he confronted me in the barn he said he was going to you, and he was going to make sure that I paid for what I did."

Bob blinked. "He was going to tell me?"

"Yes. I told him he was crazy, that you hated each other, so what was the difference? But he said he didn't hate you. He wouldn't let you lose your farm to Tyler. We argued because I knew that Tyler said if I couldn't get Nigel on our side then he had to go. I tried to convince him. He refused. So I waited until he went to the barn to get more eggs. Then I tried to talk to him again. I just wanted him to listen. I just needed him to understand that nothing had to change. He really lost it, said he was going to call the police right then. Tyler walked in and I didn't know what to do."

"And that's an excuse?" Bob roared and moved as if he might lunge towards him. At the last moment he froze. "You stood there while he killed my son!"

"Your son? You think you have the right to call him that? You threw him out of your own house!" Zac took a step towards Bob.

"Bob, please, just calm down." Ally took a few

steps towards him, but Luke moved in front of her and shot her a heated look of warning.

"Don't Ally." Luke turned his attention to Zac. "Zac, I can help you. You were involved but you didn't kill him. But if you hurt anyone here, you're going to be in more trouble than you can ever find your way out of. You have to put that poison down and put your hands up. Can you do that for me, Zac?" Luke tried to meet his eyes. His voice was so soothing that even Ally relaxed a little. But it had no impact on Zac.

"Keep quiet, you have nothing to do with any of this. I can't believe this happened." Zac reached up and wiped at his cheek.

"Careful, you might have some of that on your hands." Ally watched him closely as his body tensed.

"Oh no!" He pulled his hand away from his face. "Oh, this is all out of control. What am I going to do?"

"You're going to walk over here." The booming voice echoed through the barn.

Ally turned to see Tyler in the doorway. "Real slow, Zac, real slow."

Zac started to walk towards Tyler. "Tyler, where were you?"

"You really screwed this up now, didn't you?" Tyler shook his head. "I told you to do one thing."

"I tried!" Zac gasped out his words. "There was a pig, and then Bob, and then you took off!"

"You took too long. If you'd done what I said, then the plan would have worked. Bob would have walked in on her dead body and he would have gone to jail for the murder of his son, and this woman. Instead, we're going to have to take things in a different direction."

"What do you mean?" Zac tightened his grip on the poison. Luke kept his hand on his weapon. Ally could tell he was looking for a safe moment to take the upper hand.

Tyler looked across the barn at Bob. "I think it's time Bob gave up his land."

"Tyler, what you're doing here is going to get

you life in prison." Luke stared hard at him. "You need to just admit to your crime and let me take you in. Your plan didn't work, it's falling apart around you. Now is the time to surrender."

"No." Tyler shook his head and laughed. "I don't need to do any such thing. As far as I'm concerned, Bob found out about Nigel poisoning his crops. So he killed him. Then this little lady figured it out, so he killed her. I'll dump Bob's body where they'll never find it, they'll just think he's run away. And you." He looked directly at Luke. "You're the poor sap that tried to save her and got caught in the barn fire that Bob lit. You see how all of that works out just perfect?"

"What fire?" Ally's eyes widened. "Tyler, you can't do that. You can't."

"I can do anything I please. I'm getting the rest of this land no matter what it takes." He locked eyes with Bob. "Maybe if you had just given it to me, none of this would have ever happened."

"You're insane, Tyler. What happened to you?" Bob took a step towards him. Ally held up her hand to stop him. She didn't want him to risk being the first victim of the poison.

"What happened to me? Money Bob. That's what. I have it, and I want more of it, and I will do anything to take it. Understand?"

"Yeah, I understand. You're psychotic and a murderer, and no matter what you try to do to me, I promise you I will get revenge for my son's death."

Tyler chuckled and rolled his eyes. "Your son came to me, when you rejected him."

"And my son died defending me." Bob thrust out his chest. "What does that tell you?"

"It tells me that you're about to join him." He reached into his pocket and pulled out a lighter. "Now, if there's anything that any of you think you can do about this, think again. I've already spread the gasoline around the barn. This thing will go up in seconds. Zac and I are going to walk out of here. Aren't we, Zac?"

Zac still held the poison as tight as possible.

His hands trembled from the tension of his muscles.

"Tyler I..."

"Don't question me, or I will lock you in here with the rest of them."

Luke pulled his gun and pointed it at Tyler. "Put that lighter out." His voice was fierce as he aimed the gun.

"Cute. By the time you fire a bullet, this lighter will already be hitting the ground. Who do you think is going to win here?"

"Luke, don't." Ally walked over to him and placed her hand on the arm that wielded the gun. "Don't." She spoke in a soothing tone. Luke forced himself to look away from Tyler long enough to meet Ally's eyes.

"There's no way out, Ally," Luke said.

"Tyler! This is crazy!" Bob began to shout. "Help! Someone help us!"

"Scream all you want. No one is going to be out here at this time of night. You're not getting out of this. Let's go, Zac." He backed up towards the door. Ally saw the opportunity to subdue at least one danger.

"Zac, put down the pesticide. If you're holding it and it catches fire who knows what will happen." She met his eyes. "Put it down."

"All right." He set the bag down on the ground. Tyler backed up to the door of the barn. It was still open just a little. He grinned at the three he left behind.

"See ya around sometime, Bob." He flicked the lighter on again. Then a burst of air extinguished it. In the next moment Tyler cried out in pain. He grabbed the back of his head and sunk to his knees. When he collapsed Charlotte was revealed behind him. She held the flashlight high as if she might strike him again. Zac started to lunge at her, but Luke shouted to stop him.

"Don't do it, Zac! Don't you move!" He trained the gun between the two men. "Charlotte, get the lighter."

Charlotte snatched the lighter up off the

ground. Luke took long strides towards the two men. "Turn around and face the wall."

"Ally, come here!" Charlotte opened her arms to her granddaughter. Ally ran straight towards her. As they embraced Arnold squealed between them. The moment that she was in her grandmother's arms Ally felt a sense of relief.

"Everyone out. This place could go up too easy." Luke demanded as he kept his gun on the two criminals. Tyler slowly got to his feet. "Ally, call the Mainbry police department, let them get their guys out here to handle these two."

"Absolutely." Ally nodded.

"Here, use mine." Charlotte offered her cell phone. Charlotte, Ally, and Bob stepped out of the barn. Luke, Tyler, and Zac followed after. Ally contacted the police department. When she explained the situation they agreed to send out officers and the detective working the case. When Ally hung up the phone she spotted Bob near the road. He stared aimlessly into the dark. Charlotte took Arnold from Ally and took him to Ally's car.

She put him on the backseat to keep him safe. Ally walked over to Bob and touched his elbow lightly.

"Are you okay?"

"How can I be?" He stared at her with dazed eyes. "I never expected anything like this to happen."

"You couldn't have," Ally said. "But the important thing is that Nigel still loved you, Bob. No matter what bad blood was between you, that bond was not broken."

Bob shook his head. "If only I had never thrown him out, none of this would have happened."

"You don't know that. The only people responsible for any of this, are Tyler and Zac. Their greed would have led them to something like this eventually."

"Maybe." Bob wiped his eyes. "Now what do I do?"

Ally looked up the road at a car that drove down from the main house. "Well, you didn't have just one son who believed in you, Bob. Colin does, too. Maybe the two of you can find a way to rebuild together."

"Yes." Bob nodded as Colin's car pulled to a stop. Colin jumped out in the same moment that several patrol cars with flashing lights rolled up to the barn.

"What happened? Dad, are you okay? Ally?" He looked between the two as he ran up to them.

"I'm okay, son. I'm okay." Bob opened his arms to Colin. Colin embraced him. Ally stepped away to give them their privacy. She turned just in time to see Luke look over at her. Despite the fact that they were several feet apart she could see the shine in his eyes. She braced herself for the possibility that he would be absolutely furious with her for going to Bob's farm. He crossed the distance between them as the Mainbry police officers cuffed Zac and Tyler. When he reached her, she began to apologize.

"Luke I..."

"Sh. Don't." He coasted his palm down her

cheek and settled it on her shoulder. "You're not hurt?"

"Not too bad." She studied him with some concern. Was he so angry that he didn't want to hear any excuses?

"You should get checked out at the hospital." He took her hand.

"No, I don't want to go to the hospital, Luke." She lowered her eyes. "I know you probably think I'm a complete fool."

"No." He caught her chin and tilted her head up once more. "I would never think that about you, Ally. You're gutsy, brave, and a great investigator. You figured out what no one else could. Was it risky?" His jaw rippled with tension. "Yes, it was. But it was what you thought was right. I trust you, Ally, I trust your judgment. I just wish you hadn't been in danger."

"I'm sorry." She smiled as she looked into his eyes. "But you still saved me."

"I think in this case that honor goes to your

grandmother." Luke looked past Ally to Ally's car where Charlotte stood. "I see where you get your talents from."

"That's the truth." Ally laughed. He let his hand fall away, but his eyes lingered on hers.

"Ally, I'm not going to tell you what you already know. This was a big risk. But it was your choice. I can respect that. If..."

"If?" She searched his eyes.

"If you'll dance with me."

She glanced around at the police officers still gathered to process the scene. "Here?"

"No." He grinned. "At the dance that we have tickets for."

"Oh, the dance." Ally blinked and then broke into a wide smile. "Mee-Maw told you, didn't she?"

"Uh." Luke shrugged. "I am a good investigator too, you know."

"Will you have time to buy a suit?"

"I might have already bought one."

"You thought your chances were good?"

"Pretty good." He nodded and wrapped an arm around her shoulders. As they walked towards Ally's car, Ally's heart flipped. With his arm around her she felt safe.

"Very good." She rested her head against his shoulder.

"It's been quite an adventure tonight." Charlotte rubbed her hands together. "Who wants cookies?"

"Cookies?" Luke laughed.

"Actually, that sounds wonderful." Ally grinned. "What do you say, Luke?"

"I would, but there's going to be a ton of paperwork to file about this. I should really be available to the detective on the case if he needs any information."

"I understand." Ally hugged him and then pulled away. "Thank you, Luke."

"Always, Ally. Always." He held her gaze for a

long moment before he turned to walk back towards the police cars. "See you at the dance!" He turned back and winked at her.

"Looking forward to it." Ally blushed. Charlotte slipped her arm around Ally's.

"He's quite a find, my dear."

"Yes. He is. Isn't he?"

"Mmhm." Charlotte pulled her close again. "I'm so glad you're safe. You must have been so frightened."

"Yes, I was to be honest." Ally frowned. "I didn't expect anyone to find me. How did you find me?"

"You left us a trail of pig feed. Didn't you?"

"I can't believe you found it." Ally shook her head. "I only left it so I could find my way back because it was getting dark. I didn't expect you to find it."

"I didn't find it, but Arnold sure did."

"That poor pig must be starving."

"Not anymore. He gobbled up every bit on his way to you."

"Mee-Maw, if you hadn't shown up when you did, I don't know what would have happened."

"But I did, sweetie. That's all that matters right now. So please, don't focus on anything else." She rubbed Ally's shoulder. "Now let's go, you need to get some rest before your dance. Are you sure that you don't want to get that head checked out?"

"No, I'm fine. Just tired."

"Well, I'll drive you home."

"How did you get here?"

"I hitched a ride with Luke."

"Aha." Ally smiled at her as she opened the passenger door of the car. "Now I know how he found out about the tickets."

"Who me?" Charlotte grinned. When Ally climbed into the car Arnold began to snort and squeal. Ally stroked his head.

"My little hero. I promise to never let you get

too hungry again, Arnold. I don't care if you try to trip me or not. You're a good pig."

Arnold squealed and nuzzled her hand.

Chapter Sixteen

Ally spent the next two days at home. It took a lot to relinquish her duties to her grandmother, but she knew she needed the rest. Peaches refused to leave her side. If she was in bed, Peaches curled up next to her. If she sat on the couch, Peaches jumped right up onto her lap. Ally was grateful for the company.

Luke kept her up to date on how the case was unfolding and how both Tyler and Zac were expected to spend a long time behind bars, but she had not seen him in person. Even though she hadn't been able to see his face, she could picture his exact expressions when he texted her. She was excited to go to the dance with him. It seemed silly to her that she had been so resistant to his advances. He was an amazing person, and she didn't want to miss out on getting to know him better. However, when the night of the dance arrived, she didn't hear a word from him. She tried to call to confirm he would be there, but he didn't answer the phone. She let it go at first, but as the hours ticked by, she started to get nervous. Had he changed his mind? Had something happened to him? She dressed for the dance, but continued to wonder if she would have a date after all. When she met her grandmother at Freely Lakes Charlotte was a little surprised.

"I thought that Luke would have driven you."

"I haven't heard from him." Ally lowered her eyes. "I'm not sure if he will be here."

"I'm sure he will be. He probably got caught up on a case or something."

"You're absolutely right. I think I'll just wait out front for him, so he knows where the dance is."

"That's a good plan." Charlotte patted her arm. "My friend and I are going to check on the refreshments."

"Just when do I get to meet this friend of yours?" Ally raised an eyebrow.

"Hmm, when I'm ready." Charlotte winked at

her.

"Mee-Maw! I need to make sure this guy is worthy of your attention." Ally crossed her arms.

"Oh, that's sweet. But I happen to think that I am the best judge of that." She patted Ally's arm. "Don't worry, he'll be here." As Charlotte disappeared into the large gymnasium where the dance was to be held, Ally made her way out through the front door. She seemed to be waiting there for ages anxiously looking at everyone that was arriving, hoping it was Luke.

Ally was getting cold and decided she would leave, Luke obviously wasn't going to turn up. She pulled open the door to the recreation center so she could say good-bye to her grandmother. As she was walking inside a voice from the parking lot drew her attention.

"Ally, wait!"

She turned to look at the sound of Luke's voice. When she saw him rushing up the walkway towards her she was dazzled by how handsome he was in his suit. He straightened his tie as he slowed to a stop right in front of her. "I'm sorry I'm late." He met her eyes. "I'm really, really, sorry."

She smiled as she looked into his eyes. "All that matters is that you're here now. I wasn't sure that you would come."

"I wouldn't miss this for anything." He sighed. "I was on a case, and I left my cell phone, and I didn't have time to go back and get it because I had to pick up my suit. I should have stopped somewhere to call you, but I just really wanted to get here." He offered her his hand. "May I have this dance?"

"Absolutely. And the one after, and the one after that." She wrapped her arm around his.

"Well, then I guess we will have to warn the staff that we might never leave." He winked at her and led her into the recreation building.

It wasn't until she felt the warmth of his palm on the small of her back that she was able to relax enough to hear the music. She took his hand and expected him to leave some space between them.

Instead he pulled her right up against him and looked into her eyes.

Ally looked into his eyes and realized that she was ready for her next adventure.

The End

Chocolate Cookie Recipe

Ingredients:

4 ounces butter

4 ounces semisweet chocolate

1 1/2 cups all-purpose flour

1/2 teaspoon salt

1/2 teaspoon baking powder

2 tablespoons cocoa powder

2 large eggs

1 cup light brown sugar

1 teaspoon vanilla extract

1/3 cup white chocolate chips

1/2 cup milk chocolate chips

Preparation:

Preheat oven to 350 degrees Fahrenheit.

Place parchment paper on cookie trays.

Melt chocolate and butter over a low heat preferably in a double boiler. Leave aside to cool.

Sift flour, salt, baking powder and cocoa powder into a bowl.

Beat eggs, brown sugar and vanilla extract together.

Stir the chocolate mixture into the egg mixture.

Gradually add the dry ingredients to the wet mixture and stir until combined.

Mix in the white and milk chocolate chips. The quantity and kind of chocolate chips can be changed to suit your taste.

Leave the mixture in the fridge for about an hour so it is easy to roll.

Roll the cooled mixture into balls about the size of a tablespoon and place on the baking tray about 2 inches apart. Flatten the balls slightly. This recipe makes 24 cookies.

Bake for about 10-12 minutes and then remove from the oven. The cookies will be soft, but will continue cooking while they cool.

Leave to cool on the tray for about 10 minutes then transfer to a wire rack to cool completely.

Enjoy!

More Cozy Mysteries by Cindy Bell

Chocolate Centered Cozy Mysteries

The Sweet Smell of Murder

A Deadly Delicious Delivery

A Bitter Sweet Murder

Sage Gardens Cozy Mysteries

Birthdays Can Be Deadly

Money Can Be Deadly

Trust Can Be Deadly

Ties Can Be Deadly

Rocks Can Be Deadly

Jewelry Can Be Deadly

Numbers Can Be Deadly

Dune House Cozy Mysteries

Seaside Secrets

Boats and Bad Guys

Treasured History

Hidden Hideaways

Dodgy Dealings

Suspects and Surprises

Wendy the Wedding Planner Cozy Mysteries

Matrimony, Money and Murder

Chefs, Ceremonies and Crimes

Knives and Nuptials

Mice, Marriage and Murder

Heavenly Highland Inn Cozy Mysteries

Murdering the Roses

Dead in the Daisies

Killing the Carnations

Drowning the Daffodils

Suffocating the Sunflowers

Books, Bullets and Blooms

A Deadly serious Gardening Contest

A Bridal Bouquet and a Body

Bekki the Beautician Cozy Mysteries

Hairspray and Homicide

A Dyed Blonde and a Dead Body

Mascara and Murder

Pageant and Poison

Conditioner and a Corpse

Mistletoe, Makeup and Murder

Hairpin, Hair Dryer and Homicide

Blush, a Bride and a Body

Shampoo and a Stiff

Cosmetics, a Cruise and a Killer

Lipstick, a Long Iron and Lifeless

Camping, Concealer and Criminals

Treated and Dyed

Made in the USA
Monee, IL
28 January 2023

26533251R00138